CW01563918

For All
Eternity

For All Eternity

DEE AYRES

TATE PUBLISHING
AND ENTERPRISES, LLC

For All Eternity
Copyright © 2014 by Dee Ayres. All rights reserved.

No part of this publication may be reproduced, stored in a retrieval system or transmitted in any way by any means, electronic, mechanical, photocopy, recording or otherwise without the prior permission of the author except as provided by USA copyright law.

The opinions expressed by the author are not necessarily those of Tate Publishing, LLC.

This novel is a work of fiction. Names, descriptions, entities, and incidents included in the story are products of the author's imagination. Any resemblance to actual persons, events, and entities is entirely coincidental.

Published by Tate Publishing & Enterprises, LLC
127 E. Trade Center Terrace | Mustang, Oklahoma 73064 USA
1.888.361.9473 | www.tatepublishing.com

Tate Publishing is committed to excellence in the publishing industry. The company reflects the philosophy established by the founders, based on Psalm 68:11,
"The Lord gave the word and great was the company of those who published it."

Book design copyright © 2014 by Tate Publishing, LLC. All rights reserved.
Cover design by Rodrigo Adolfo
Interior design by Joana Quilantang

Published in the United States of America

ISBN: 978-1-63367-450-9
Fiction / Romance / General
Fiction / Christian / Romance
14.08.27

To Roy, who always supported and encouraged my dreams. The man who until the day he went home to God, showed me every day that I was loved by always kissing me good-bye, by simply holding my hand at every opportunity and by just telling me at least once a day that he loved me. Unconditional love, God's blessing to all of us, enjoy it, share it.

PROLOGUE

"Those two have had three years together. You would have thought that by now they would have realized that their destiny was in each other."

"Well, Charlie, He never said our assignments would be easy. You know those two have been leading us on a merry dance since the day they were born, and I suspect these next few won't be an easier."

"You're right, Sid. Do you remember her fifth birthday? Nearly cost me my wings when she climbed up into that apple tree, simply because some bully told her that babies could not climb trees and that she was still a baby. It was a good thing that she was wearing those overalls, so that way, I could get that branch tangled up in the strap to keep her safe until her father came."

"I remember that. It was the same year that Derek turned ten and tried to make it his last year on earth. Just because his older brother, Adam, helped their father break in the new untamed horses that year while he was not. Up to that point, I had never seen Kevin Callahan so angry or scared as when he found his middle son on top of his newest wild stallion heading for the open field. It was a good thing that horse listened to reason about jumping that five-foot fence."

"Charlie, I think you've got it. You're right. These two hardheads need a special kind of push. I think I might have an idea, although the Boss might not be too happy."

"Well, He's not going to be too happy if we don't get these two back on schedule. So let's hear your idea."

"Well, didn't they say something about going with their friends to Las Vegas to stand up with them at their wedding?"

"Yes, how is that going to help our cause?"

"All we need to do is…" Sid began.

The stars in the sky twinkled a little bit brighter as they reflected the laughter of two conspiring angels.

1

Derek ran his hand through his hair and around the back of his neck, as if somehow the rubbing would ease the pain of the headache, which throbbed unceasingly. He had already called for room service to bring up juice and pain relievers. When there was finally a knock on the door, Derek let the paper he had been trying to read flutter back down to the table and went to let the bellboy in. With a gesture to remain quiet, Derek gave the runner a tip and took the tray from him. After quietly closing the door, he set the tray down. Then with a grateful prayer, he helped himself to both the juice and the pain relievers before pouring a second glass of juice and shaking out a couple more aspirin tablets into his hand. Turning, he looked over to the bed where Tracey lay sleeping. "Okay, Tracey, it is time for you to wake up and join me in this nightmare."

Sitting down on the side of the bed, Derek reached out to brush the soft silky strands of hair away from her face with his free hand. As he admired the golden-red tresses that looked like molten lava over the pillows, he whispered quietly, "Tracey, Tracey, why do you always keep this beautiful hair pulled into a braid or twisted into a knot?"

When his soft touches began to make her stir into wakefulness, he pulled his hand away and stood up. As he stood next to the bed watching her wake up, he realized that this was one case where discretion was the better part of valor. "Oh, honey, I have a feeling that you are going to have a harder time with all this than I did." Again, he spoke softly, wondering how to make this easier for her. He still had not come to an appropriate solution by the time Tracey's eyes fluttered open.

Tracey slowly opened her eyes and then shut them immediately, as the light caused an excruciating pain to shoot through her head. She moaned softly. However, even that little movement, and sound ricochet off her skull like a bomb. Shielding her eyes, as well as holding her head, she rolled over onto her back. She could not remember ever having a headache like this before. "Did someone get the license of the truck that hit me?" she murmured aloud, not actually expecting an answer.

"No, it was moving too fast over me at the time. However, if you ask nice, I might be persuaded to give you these aspirins in my hand."

Startled at the sound of Derek's voice, Tracey's eyes flew open. Sitting up, she looked around until she spotted him leaning against the bedpost at the foot of the bed.

"You! What are you doing in my room?" she demanded angrily and then grabbed her head as the pounding intensified.

"Yes, it's me, and currently, I am here trying to give you some aspirin for that apparent hangover of yours," he told her. Then some mischievous demon in him decided to add, "And if you must know, you are in my room, not the other way around."

Holding tight to her head, she looked around and found that he was right. It was his room. She suddenly had so many questions she wanted to ask, but first, she needed the aspirin in his hand. She would have liked to refuse just on principle, but something told her she was going to need all the strength she could muster before she found the answers to the questions currently sounding off in her head.

"Sorry," she apologized for her accusation as she stretched out her hand palm up for the aspirin. With a smile, Derek placed the tablets in her hand and then handed her the juice after she popped them into her mouth. "Thank you," she told him as she handed him back the half-empty glass. It was then she first noticed the sheet once covering her had dropped to her waist when she sat up.

Her face flamed red when she realized she was stark naked and totally exposed to Derek. Quickly, she snatched the sheet back up to cover herself and looked around the room for her clothes. Finally, she spied them lying over a chair by the window. His tie lay on her dress while her stockings tangled with his socks. Even their shoes were tumbled together. "Oh no, we couldn't have." Lying back down, she covered her head with the sheet, hoping to block out the incriminating evidence.

"Oh, yes, I do believe we did," Derek told her with a small chuckle, finding humor in the situation for the first time since he had awoken this morning.

"Go away."

"Oh, I don't think so, because I do think we need to discuss this situation through, don't you?"

"No, I don't. I do not think it is a good idea at all. I will tell you what though, you go away, and I will go back to sleep until I can get rid of this headache. Then when I wake up, we can just pretend this was a nightmare and let it go to the way it was before," she told him. She lay down and covered her head with the sheet.

Derek had felt much the same way when he had realized whom it was that he had spent the night with; however, watching his unflappable, always-in-control executive assistant come unglued at the seams, he was finding her more desirable than ever. As he sat beside her, he tugged on the sheet covering her head.

"Sorry, honey, but I don't think hiding will make the reality of last night just go away."

"I can't hear you. I'm sleeping, and you are just a figment in my most current nightmare."

"Tracey, we apparently got a little too close last night, and there are possible repercussions, ones that will be no figment to anyone's imagination."

"I can't hear you. I'm sleeping," she chanted repeatedly until, with a sigh, Derek pulled the sheet away from her head, laughing as she kept her eyes closed and continued to pretend to ignore him.

"I never did like being ignored," he told her just before lowering his mouth to hers.

Tracey raised her arms to push him away, and somehow, they involuntarily wrapped around his neck, letting him get even closer.

"I always did like the story of Sleeping Beauty," he murmured against her lips, then deepened the kiss once more before pulling back. "Still sleeping?"

His words brought her out of his spell and back into reality with a thud. "I hate you."

"You know what they say hate is akin to, don't you?" He gave her a knowing look that had her swallowing a repeat of the words. "Good. Now, battling is not getting us anywhere, and to tell you the truth, I would rather expend the energy trying to figure out what happened last night. It's all a little fuzzy to me. What about you?"

Humor the man, and maybe he will go away, she thought to herself. Therefore, she settled back against the pillows, making sure she secured the sheet around herself, an action which brought a smile to Derek's face. "So what do you want to know?" she asked.

"I want to know exactly what you remember about yesterday, because since neither of us drink, how could we both have apparent hangovers and memory loss?"

"I never thought about that," she stated, realizing for the first time that he was right; something was definitely strange. She thought about the previous day for a moment before she started to speak, "Okay, I remember that I left San Diego with Susan, and the arrangements were that you were to ride in with Rick. Once we arrived here in Las Vegas, I went shopping with Susan for a few needed essentials while you men were checking us into our rooms and then doing who knows what. Susan's parents were to finalize the last small details for the reception before joining Susan and I to get dressed for the wedding. When the time came, we went down to the limousine and went to the chapel. After they got married, we went to the reception. We had dinner and then the small band they hired played a-and…" She stammered a moment, not wanting to remember dancing with him and maybe admitting inadvertently how it had made her feel.

Therefore, Tracey sidestepped the issue with, "Everyone was dancing. After that, I"— she stopped at that point because the memories stopped—"I can't remember anything else." She looked up at him with tears shimmering in her eyes. The feeling of being totally out of control scared her.

"That's about the point I lose it too," he told her. However, he also had the additional memory of their friends teasing them about the chemistry between them, offering to return them to the chapel so they could legally put that chemistry to work. Derek figured Tracey would not appreciate that particular memory, so he did not share it. "Anyway, nothing explains our lack of memory about last night. The strongest thing we drank was that fruit punch they had on the buffet table. And I don't take drugs." He paused for a moment, thinking, but Tracey took that pause personally.

"I don't take drugs either, you know, and I am sure I didn't drug you."

"I didn't mean it that way, honey, I—" Derek began quickly.

"And *don't* call me honey. I am not your honey," Tracey interrupted.

"I—" he tried again, but she interrupted again. This time, he could tell she was working up a head of steam.

"Mr. Callahan—" she started, but this time, he interrupted her. "Tracey, I think we are past the Mr. Callahan and Ms. Conway stage, don't you think?" He indicated the room with a sweep of his hand.

"Mr. Callahan," she began again, ignoring him, and went on as she held her throbbing head, "I think rehashing this is futile. Something happened to us, something we will probably never know or understand. I say we just forget everything, what may or may not have happened. Someone thought putting us in here together was some kind of joke, unfunny as it is, but it's over. So now if you just get your things and go away, I can get up and get dressed. Then we can head back to San Diego. Tomorrow is a workday." To her mind, if they ignored this particular problem, it would just go away.

Tracey realized that Derek did not intend to make this easy for her when he stood up and leaned back against the bedpost.

"If you want to get up and get dressed, go right ahead," he taunted her with a wave of his hand toward their entangled clothes.

"Will you please get out?"

"No."

"No? This is ridiculous. Then at least turn around," she demanded in exasperation as she began to wiggle her way to the side of the bed, trying desperately to keep the sheet protectively around her.

"No."

Tracey's head dropped into her hand as she shook it slowly. "Mr. Callahan, I do not know what has gotten into you. Maybe whatever put us here in the first place has not gotten fully out of your system, but I am tired. My head feels like there's an amtrac train running through it at full speed, and I am thoroughly disgusted with this whole business. I have been your account executive for the last two years, as well as your executive assistant for the year before that. In all that time, even though you were constantly exhausting and irritating, you have never been totally unreasonable."

"Thank you, I think?" Derek was not sure that what she had said was a compliment.

"Until now," she clarified. "Will you please just go away for about an hour and give me some privacy to pull myself together?"

"No."

"Are you serious? Why not?"

"Because," Derek began as he stepped forward and pulled her to her feet. Then he reached down to pull her left hand into view. "What new husband do you know who gives his wife privacy to get out of bed on their honeymoon?"

The sheet she had been wearing slipped unnoticed to the floor as her eyes focused for the first time on the shiny gold wedding band on her finger. Then she heard him add, "Mrs. Callahan."

Tracey stared out of the airplane's window, her still-throbbing head resting against the cool glass. *This has got to be a nightmare or a bad joke of some kind. I cannot be married to that horrible man. No way, no how. I hate him.*

Do you? The question seemed to come at her from out of nowhere.

Of course I hate him. He's everything I do not want in a man.

You do not want a successful, hardworking man? Charlie asked as he shook his head in frustration at her stubbornness.

Well, that's not it. He's a workaholic. He has no time for relationships. I have watched him over the years. As soon as a woman gets too close or wants more in their relationship, he pushes them away. He sends them a dozen roses and a Dear

Jane card, or else they give up on him and his sixteen-hour days, Tracey answered.

Maybe he just hasn't found the right person to go home to. Someone who might make him take time for a relationship. What else don't you like about him? His looks? His tall, six-foot-four-inch frame? His big strong shoulders? The light brown hair doesn't go well with his gray eyes?

Okay, so he's good- looking in a rough and rugged sort of way. Even so, looks are not everything.

So I guess he doesn't have a sense of humor? Grouchy or angry all the time? He never laughs? Charlie pushed her to admit her true feelings.

Well, he does a wicked sense of the ridiculous, Tracey admitted.

Well then, he must hate kids and animals.

He has a Saint Bernard named Barney, and he adores his little niece.

His kisses must repulse you?

They turn me to jelly. I can't think straight when he gets too close.

So let's get this straight. Derek Callahan is a tall good-looking hunk of a man with a wicked sense of humor, works hard, loves kids and dogs. He makes you go weak in the knees, and you hate him.

Yes.

Right, Charlie said as he rolled his eyes in absolute frustration.

Shut up. Tracey closed her eyes. *Great, he's got me arguing with myself, and I can't even win that argument. I am in big trouble here.*

When the plane touched down in San Francisco, Tracey quickly gathered her things. When she had run from the hotel, she had gone straight to the airport and booked the first available flight to San Francisco, home to the only person she could even think of that would understand and help her fix this mess—her father.

$$\sim$$

The five-hour drive from Las Vegas to the family ranch in San Diego did nothing to cool Derek's temper.

"I cannot believe she left. With so much left to discuss, she runs off. Well, that is the last time I take pity on her. I mean the woman practically faints when she finds out we got married. Therefore, when she begged for a little time to adjust, I gave it to her. I took an extra long shower and took my time shaving. So what do I get for my trouble? An empty room, that's what I get. Just wait until I get my hands on her. I'm either going to strangle her or give her the spanking she apparently missed out on as a child." Derek ranted aloud as he drove.

"Or kiss her?" Sid queried as he tried not to laugh.

"Why would I kiss that stubborn little witch?" Derek demanded of his unseen passenger.

"Because you have never felt as complete as you do when she is in your arms."

"No way! Things are just fine the way they are. Besides, she doesn't want anything to do with me."

"Are you sure about that?"

"I'm as certain as one can be when she leaves the word *annulment* written on the bedroom mirror before running away from me."

"So you are going to give up on the only woman you have ever really wanted? The one you compare the entire female population to?"

"Want her? Are you nuts? She is not my type."

"*You're right. She's much too smart and independent. You need a simpering doormat to come home to, one who will listen and agree to everything you have to say.*"

"Well, no, that type bores me. Tracey is loyal and dependable, as well as a stimulating conversationalist. She also keeps me on my toes, constantly. It's nice to know I can count on her to get a job done or to be able to make competent decisions when I am away."

"*Okay, so she's loyal, dependable, and she stimulates your mind both personally and professionally. Therefore, she must not stimulate your other senses. It's the hair. Must be the hair. Much too brassy red, right? Or maybe it's her dark blue eyes. Aren't redheads supposed to have green eyes? And did you see those freckles this morning? It's no wonder she keeps them hidden under makeup. Besides, at five feet four, she is much too short for you.*" Sid pushed him harder, trying to get Derek to admit his true feelings.

"Her hair is not brassy. It's a golden red. It shimmers like silk, and it's amazingly soft to the touch. Green eyes are typical and ordinary for a redhead. Her eyes are like blue velvet. They darken adoringly whenever I pull her into my arms and sparkle whenever she laughs. As for those freckles, they are adorable. I never want her to cover them again. They remind me of a story I once heard about angel kisses being scattered on her nose by her guardian angels. As for her size, she fits against me just perfectly."

"*Okay, so you apparently like her looks. It must be that she is cold and unfeeling, not caring for anyone but herself.*"

"I have seen her constantly giving to others without a thought of reward. She works every holiday season at the homeless shelters. Everyone in the office goes to her with their problems because they know she will listen and keep their confidence. She only seems distant and cold when I try to get too close to her personally."

"She hates kids and dogs?"

"I don't think so. I have caught her playing with Barney on many occasions when I brought him into the office on Saturdays. Furthermore, she has several nephews she adores and goes home to see as often as she can."

"So what you are saying is that Tracey Conway Callahan is a beautiful, warm, and passionate woman who loves kids and pets, the one woman who can stimulate your mind and your body, but she's not for you."

"Yes."

"Right."

"Shut up."

Derek pulled to a stop in front of the family ranch house and got out, slamming the door behind him.

"Well, Charlie, I think we are beginning to make some progress. What do you think?"

"I think we have a long way to go, Sid, a really long way to go."

2

"So, little brother, what are you going to do about your runaway bride?" Adam asked Derek after he had heard what he now dubbed as the Great Vegas Story.

"I swear, if you laugh just once more, I'm going to pound you into the ground," Derek threatened. Then he slumped down into his chair. "To tell you the truth, I have no idea what I am going to do."

"Did you pray for guidance? What does your gut instinct tell you to do?" Adam asked him the same questions their father had always asked whenever the boys had been in a dilemma over something.

"Of course I prayed, but all my gut instinct is telling me to do is to strangle her," he answered with a grin; Adam just shook his head and waited for the real answer.

"Oh, all right. What I really want to do is find her, bring her back, and then after I strangle her, make this marriage a reality."

"Then why are you still sitting here? Get going."

"Easier said than done. She didn't exactly jump for joy over the news of our marriage. Besides, in the last three years, she has at no time given one indication that she is even interested in having me in her life, at least on a personal level. In fact, she avoids me whenever possible. Do you know she has never called me by my first name? Mind you, this should not have been the case since our best friends met each other last year and began dating. I mean, we have been to so many social functions together that it looked to most people that we were double dating."

"She married you."

"She was either too drunk or drugged to know better. I have more memories of the evening than she does, and it is still really fuzzy to me."

"Come on now, Derek, you know as well as I do that no one will go against their natural instincts, even if they are drunk, drugged, or hypnotized. Subconsciously, you two married each other because you wanted to."

"Sure she did. That's why when she found out we were married, she darn near fainted and then, at the first opportunity, ran for the hills."

"A natural reaction I would say. I love ya, but I have felt that way around you myself a time or two." Adam grinned at his brother, who just scowled back at him.

"Oh, you are such a funnyman. Okay, let's just say for argument's sake you are right. How do you propose I get my *wife* to agree that she's all in favor of this marriage?"

"Just use those famous powers of persuasion skills you are known for. Look, Derek, if you can create a multimillion dollar company, you have the ability to convince one small lady to reveal her true feelings for you and then make it last."

Before Derek could answer, Adam's eighteen-month-old daughter, Amanda, came toddling into the room and headed straight for Derek.

"Unc Ric, Unc Ric!" Amanda called out happily, lifting her arms to her uncle.

"Hello, princess. How's my favorite girl?" Derek nuzzled her soft, sweet-smelling neck, making her giggle.

Amanda reached up and placed her tiny chubby hands on his cheeks and gave him a smacking kiss. "Luv ya," she chanted at him.

"That would be her new trick," Adam informed him with a grin.

"See? What do I need with a stubborn, hot-tempered woman when I have the 'luv' of a good woman already, right, little princess? You're my girl, aren't you?"

"No, because this is the current woman of my heart. Besides, the hot tempered woman you are ranting about is the only one that will make you whole. She's the one that will give you the chance at having one of these." Adam indicated the baby cuddled against his chest. "She's your chance at having it all."

"Okay, I'll go find the little witch, but I have a feeling I would be better off if I just let you shoot me and put me out my misery."

"I would never shoot you, little brother, but if that cop friend of yours has an extra bulletproof vest, I would suggest borrowing it."

"Why?"

"Because didn't the marriage vows say something like 'til death do us part'?"

"I don't remember," Derek ground out just before slamming the front door on the sound of Adam's laughter.

Three days later, Tracey was still with her family in San Francisco. She had wired her resignation in to the company by eight on Monday morning, less than twenty-four hours after her arrival.

"I still cannot believe you are taking the coward's way out. You never have before," Robert chided his daughter.

"I am not a coward. I have legitimate vacation time coming, as well as over two weeks of accrued sick time. I am just using a little of it up in lieu of working out my notice."

"You are running away, and at some point, you are going to have to be honest with yourself. Until then, daughter of mine, I am going inside to work on the Carmichael's case," Robert said as he dropped a kiss on the tip of her nose. As he went into the house, his eldest daughter, Ann, stepped out. Robert shook his head, letting Ann know that he had not gotten anywhere with her younger sister.

"Hey, little sister, what's on the schedule today? Are you planning on indulging in some more moping and crying or maybe just a little self-pity?" Ann, Tracey's older sister, asked.

"Was it marriage or motherhood that helped refine your sense of humor?" Tracey questioned sarcastically.

"Both." Ann smiled, and Tracey felt an answering smile tugging at her lips. "Well, that's much better. Now, little sister, how can I help?"

"You can help me convince Dad to get the paperwork filed for the annulment and represent me in my absence."

"I'd love to, but I happen to agree with Dad. You love this man. Why would you want to annul your marriage to him?"

"I do not love that man. He's—"

"He's the man of your dreams."

"He's the man of my nightmares."

"Liar. You talk about him all the time. Every time you start dating a man, you compare them to him."

"I do not compare anyone to him on a personal basis. I might compare or talk about him because he's a savvy businessman, and I learn a lot from him."

"Tracey, I am your sister, and no matter how far apart we are, we have always been close. We share secrets and support one another through everything, so don't start trying to lie to me now."

"Ann, I would never lie to you. I just can't let myself think of him in any other way but as a savvy businessman."

"Tracey, there is only one thing you need to ask yourself."

"And that would be?"

"Do you love him?"

Tracey just looked at her sister; tears were shimmering in her eyes. However, before she could say or do anything further, her eight-year-old nephew, Stephen, came running up to them. "Mom, Aunt Tracey, our ball is up in the tree. And I can't get it down because of the cast on my arm, but Johnnie is trying to climb up to get it."

Tracey placed her hand on her sister's arm when she would have jumped to her feet. "I'll get this one. You never were any good at tree climbing."

"And you were always good at getting out of things you didn't want to deal with."

"I have no idea what you are talking about," Tracey said innocently, blinking away the unshed tears before turning to her nephew with a smile. "Let's go save your brother and get your ball, my wounded soldier."

"I could do it you know if I didn't have this cast on."

"I am very sure you could, but didn't you get that cast jumping your skateboard off a wall?"

"Yeah."

"Then I think you have been brave enough for this month. Actually, more than enough for a year or two, as far as your mother is concerned."

"Yeah, she told me. But she's a girl, and she doesn't understand that a guy can't be a sissy, you know."

"Oh, I know," she answered as they reached the tree in question. She reached up to pluck her four-year-old nephew from the lowest branches. "Down you go, little monkey."

"Aww, Aunt Tracey."

"Sorry, chum. I'll tell you what though, I'll do the climbing, and you go where the ball is and catch it when I knock it down."

"You know how to climb a tree?" Serious doubt was evident in her nephew's voice.

"Yes."

"Are you sure?" Johnny asked, as if he needed to clarify the situation for her. "You are a girl, you know."

"Okay, you little chauvinist, girls can climb trees too. Now go get ready to catch the ball."

Slowly and carefully, she began the climb. "You're almost there, Aunt Tracey, just a bit higher and over to the right," Stephen said, guiding her from below.

"Yeah, right," she muttered to herself as she continued to climb to the higher branches. "I remember this being a lot quicker and easier when I was a kid." Finally, with a sigh of relief, she spotted the ball, and with a last stretch, she managed to free the ball and let it fall to the ground. She could tell from the fading shouts of her nephews that they had retrieved the ball and gone off to play. "At least there won't be any witnesses to my less-than-graceful descent." She laughed at herself as she began to climb back down the tree.

One minute she was going from branch to branch, and then the next thing she knew, she was stuck. "What?" Twisting around, she tried to see what had snagged her. It appeared to be a small limb tangled up in the belt loop of her jeans.

"Great, if I let go of this branch, I'll be able to get free of the limb, but I'll go crashing to the ground. So if I do not want fall and break my stupid neck, I need an extra hand in order to break free. Okay, Lord, have you ever thought about making people with three arms?" she asked in the general direction of the sky. "I guess that silence means no. Fine, I'll just figure a way out of this myself." For the next few minutes, she wiggled and squirmed, trying to pull free while still trying to stay balanced, but that little twig appeared to be unbreakable.

"You wouldn't be needing an extra hand, would you?"

Tracey jerked around in surprise, and she would have fallen if Derek hadn't pulled her up against him before reaching around her to easily break the tiny limb that had held her so securely. "Mmm, talk about a captive audience," he teased.

"What are you doing here? How did you find me? Why did you come?" She asked all three questions in one breath.

"I'm here to find you, Your personnel records, and I felt we had some unfinished business to discuss," he answered her questions in order before adding, "A discussion that would probably be easier with our feet on the ground. Although if you prefer, we can just stay up here and talk. I have no objections to holding you in my arms for a while longer."

"Let me go!" she demanded. Why was it that he was always the one to find her in such embarrassing positions? It was a habit she seemed to be developing a talent for lately.

"Oh, all right, for the moment. Grab the branch there to the right and steady yourself before I let go." Once she had done as he had asked, he made short work of climbing down the rest of the way and turned to lift her down as she came into reach.

This time, he let her slide down the length of his body but stopped her short of actually touching the ground. "Aren't you going to thank me for saving your life?"

"My life was not in danger, at least it wasn't until you tried scaring the living daylights out of me."

"Boy, are you stubborn. How about you thank me for saving your life, and I'll apologize for scaring you half to death." He offered that compromise and then dropped a kiss on her lips "I'm sorry."

"Put me down right now!" she demanded as she pushed against his chest.

"Where is my kiss for saving you?"

"Go to—" she began, but Derek covered her lips with his, effectively swallowing her words. However, he realized her anger was a different matter when she began hitting and kicking him.

"Hey, you little wildcat. Stop that or I'll turn you over my knee," he threatened.

"You wouldn't dare."

"Are you willing to chance it?"

Tracey was saved from answering his threat when two of her nephews arrived. Mikey, who was her youngest nephew, was tugging at Derek's shirt. Derek reluctantly let Tracey slide to the ground before kneeling down to Mikey's four-year-old level.

"Whatcha doin' to my aunt Tracey?"

"I was helping your aunt Tracey out of the tree. She had gotten stuck."

"Is Aunt Tracey hurt? Were you kissing her better?"

"You could put it that way, but she's okay now."

"That's good. I was just checkin' because my mommy doesn't want Aunt Tracey to be unhappy anymore. We came to make her laugh. Aunt Tracey is a lot of fun when she laughs, but last night, when we came over, I hearded her crying."

Tracey stepped forward to muzzle her young nephew before he could do any more damage, but he already had Derek looking up at her with questions in his eyes. However, before she had to come up with something to say, Stephen came running up.

"Hey, Aunt Tracey, are you okay? Is this guy bothering you?" Stephen asked in a protective tone as he stepped between his aunt and the tall man who had stood up when he arrived.

"I'm fine, Stephen. Stephen, this is Derek Callahan, my ex-boss," she introduced them, ignoring the narrowing of Derek's eyes. "Mr. Callahan, this is my oldest nephew, Stephen. This little monkey is Mikey, and the one giving you death glares from the patio is Johnnie."

Derek held out his hand to Stephen, who reluctantly accepted it. "Nice to meet you Stephen," Derek said as he shook the young man's hand.

"You too, sir," Stephen answered, but his tone said he was not ready to be happy meeting this man.

"Stephen, could you go let Grandpa know Mr. Callahan is here?" Tracey asked.

"Will you be okay with him?" Stephen pointed a finger at Derek.

"He's annoying, but he will not hurt me," she said with her tongue in cheek.

Derek realized that the young man was not about to take his aunt's word about his trustworthiness, so he stepped back and away from Tracey, immediately noting the ease in the boy's stance. "You know, I appreciate your concern for your aunt. Like you, I wouldn't want anything to happen to her. What happened to your arm? A baseball injury? You're into baseball, aren't you?"

"Yeah, but the regular season's over. My arm was a skateboard accident. The doc says it will be much better by the time the next baseball season starts up again, although I am going to miss the Fourth of July game we always play at the park before the fireworks. You play baseball?"

"I played from Little League to college. I just play for fun now. Maybe one of these days you can come down to my family's ranch and stay around. My brothers and I like to get up a good game occasionally."

"Do you really live on a ranch?"

Tracey stepped forward and turned her nephew away from Derek's charm. "Stephen, go get Grandpa, please."

"Okay, but—"

"It's okay, Stephen. I only came to talk to your aunt, and I do not intend to harm her. I promise."

"Honest?"

"Honest."

"Okay," Stephen gave in after one last assessing glance at Derek, but he still started yelling for his grandfather before he had even gone three feet, and he continued to yell all the way into the house.

"I suppose all that yelling is for my benefit?"

"Oh yes, they are very protective, and they want you to know that they are not far away, and neither is their grandfather."

"You're a close family. It's nice to see."

"We are also an honest one, and lying to my nephews is not appreciated."

"I never lied."

"You led them to believe that they would be able to come down to the ranch. That is not going to happen, especially because once I get you out of here, I won't be seeing you anymore. I don't work for you, remember?"

"I didn't lie to them. I intend to have my nephews down to visit. They need to get to know the rest of the family. And"—he paused—"your resignation was voided out when I notified the lawyer of our marriage, as you are now my partner in the architecture division of the company, not my employee."

"What?" she asked, turning to look at him in astonishment.

"Close your mouth, honey. You might catch a fly or something. Besides, we can get to all of that later. Your father is coming. Would you prefer to sit out here under our tree and talk or move back onto the patio? Your choice."

"I guess the option of handing this to the lawyers while you go back to San Diego and I stay here is out of the question?"

"What do you think?" he said as he reached out to place an arm around her waist.

"Don't touch me. I can't think straight when you touch me," she told him and then wished she could take the words back. As that was impossible, she just prayed he wouldn't read too much into them.

"At least I'm making some progress," he said.

So much for prayer.

As Tracey approached her father, she got an idea and walked a little faster. On the pretense of giving her father a hug, she whispered into his ear, "Dad, can you handle him? I'll go on into the house and leave it to you to tell him the plan. Call me when he goes." She dropped a kiss on his cheek and started to move away, heading for the house.

"No," her father told her, effectively stopping her in her tracks.

"Dad, please." She turned pleading eyes on her father, who appeared unmoved by her plea.

"Trying to run away again?" Derek asked as he stepped up on the patio.

"From you? Yes."

"All I want to do is talk. I've never known you to be afraid to talk to me before. I guess there's a first time for everything," he said, deliberately issuing a challenge.

"I am not afraid of you. Oh, just forget it. If you want to talk about nothing, then I'll humor you." She held her head up proudly, walked over to the patio table, and lowered herself into the chair farthest away.

Not that that stopped either man. Both came around the table to sit on either side of her. Suddenly, she felt trapped.

"So talk. Then you can leave." The best defense is offense, she decided, but that bravado was definitely short-lived.

"Are all your children this temperamental?" Derek asked his father-in-law.

"Pretty much, although this one is probably by far the worst."

"You must have the patience of a saint. I don't see a gray hair on your head, and I know for a fact that in just the last three days, she's given me several," Derek said as he moved his chair a little closer to Tracey and then settled back.

"Grecian formula," Robert said, his eyes twinkling as he patted his dark black hair.

"Very funny, Dad. First off, I would appreciate it if you two would not talk about me as if I wasn't here, unless you would prefer it that way, and then I would happy to oblige you both." She raised her eyebrows in question, but both men just shook their head at her. "Then, Dad, just tell him what our options are and then he can choose one and then be on his way."

"Well, honey, it's not going to be quite that simple," Robert told his daughter.

"Why? What's not simple? Someone slipped us something, we got married, we get an annulment, and we go our separate ways."

"Well, there is only one scenario that is actually appropriate for an annulment in your case. That scenario would be that both parties are willing and the marriage was never consummated."

"That's fine. In the first place, neither of us wanted this marriage, so we're willing. Secondly, in this day and age, how can consummation be proven?"

"If the woman is still a virgin, then it is pretty conclusive. Other than that, the judge would have to decide if the couple was telling the truth. Can you honestly say your marriage was not consummated?"

Tracey decided that if someone could actually die from embarrassment, she would be the next victim. She never thought she would be talking about her love life with her father. Without looking at either man, she answered as evasively as she could, "We were way too out of it, Dad. We couldn't even remember getting married, but I would have to believe that two passed out people could not do anything."

"What do you think, Derek?" Robert turned to Derek.

"Sorry, honey, but I have to disagree with you. I am not willing because I strongly believe that the marriage was consummated," Derek answered honestly.

"How can you say that? You couldn't know. You have no memory of that night!" Tracey turned on him in anger.

"Are you willing to have the exam that will prove conclusively that it didn't? Are you so sure you are still a virgin?"

"What makes you so sure I was one before Saturday night? If I wasn't, my *willingness* to have an exam or not is a moot point." Tracey returned, but she could feel her face flush with heat, and she completely avoided looking at her father.

"Were you?" Derek queried.

"That is none of your business," she told him as she sat back in her chair, as if to get further away from him.

He decided he needed to remind her of who she was now. "Of course it's my business, and a very reasonable question to ask my wife."

"Okay, children, let's just say that form of annulment is out of the question. The second option would be if one party deliberately deceived the other party and married under false pretenses. That one is usually for financial gain. So again, it's not an option for you."

"So you are telling us that an annulment is out of the question. What's left?"

"Divorce."

"Oh great, I get to be the first one in my family to be divorced. And to top it off, when people ask how long I was married, I can tell them, 'Oh, about twelve hours.' Well, fine, if that is our only option, draw up the papers and let's get on with it. Now if we are done here," she said. She had begun to rise from her chair when both men reached out, placing a hand on each of her arms, preventing her escape.

"Wait." Her father continued, "Divorce takes either an agreement by both parties that there are irreconcilable differences, and you two have not been married long enough to have this problem. Neither do you have the grounds for the option of pressing charges of a wrongdoing to one another, such as affairs and abuse."

"So what are you telling us? That we are married, and there is no way out of this mess?"

"Well, not exactly. There is another option." Robert looked at Derek and sat back to let him take over the conversation.

"Tracey. I am not going to agree to the annulment of a marriage that I believe was consummated, which and may have repercussions. Although that is only one of the two options open to us. The other option your father is talking about is for us to stay married and try to make it work."

"You have got to be kidding."

"No."

"Oh, Dad, please tell me you are not in agreement with this man. He's crazy."

Robert loved all his children dearly, and with Tracey being his youngest, he had a hard time denying her any-thing, but he knew that sometimes, the way to show her his love was to deny her what she *thought* she wanted. That way, he could give her what she really wanted. "It's the best thing, sweetheart. Think of it as a challenge. You like challenges. Find the things that you like and admire about one another and build on it."

"Never."

"Never is a long time, princess," her father cau-tioned her.

Angry tears sprang into Tracey's eyes as she jumped to her feet. Turning on Derek in her anger, she spoke with quiet determination, "I'll find a way out of this, no matter what." With that said, she ran from the patio into the house.

"Well, that wasn't too bad." Robert grinned at Derek.

"Yeah, my head is still attached to my neck." Derek grinned back at Robert, and they both added at the same time, "For now."

"Can't these two just kiss and make up? And get on with the life they are supposed to be leading?"

"Now, Charlie, you know that would be too easy, and since when has anything with these two been worry-free?"

3

All her life, whenever she was hurt or angry, she had found comfort in her room, until now. Now she paced the room, picking up everything in her path as if it would give her answers and putting them down when they didn't. That is how Ann found her, talking to her old stuffed dog.

"Are they insane or what?" she was asking the scruffy old toy.

"If you're expecting an answer to that, I'd say you have slipped over the edge."

"Oh, Ann, did you hear what they want me to do?"

"Yes."

"Please don't tell me you agree with them."

"Tracey, look at it as an opportunity to be with the man of your heart."

"You mean the man tricked into marrying me. The one who's desire to stay with me is out of a sense of obligation."

"He never said that."

"Yes, he did. He said he was unwilling to get an annulment because of what may or may not have happened the other night. His ethics and honorable ways have been his ticket to success in business, so he thinks he has to do this."

Ann knew from experience that arguing with her stubborn sister was useless. At least until something actually proved her wrong, Tracey would not change her opinion.

"Well, no matter what the reasons are, he wants to stay married. He is not going to go along with your plans, so what are you going to do now?"

"I'm not sure, but I am not going to go meekly along with their plans," Tracey told her sister, tears of frustration in her eyes. "I just know that I can't live with him for a year and then casually walk away."

"Why?"

A tear slipped down Tracey's cheek as she admitted, "Because it would break my heart."

Ann hugged her sister tightly. "Have faith, Tracey." Their family had unfailingly believed that God would always take care of them as long as they kept their faith and trust in him.

Tracey pulled away. "I have faith, Ann, but the Lord also said that he helps those who help themselves. So I need to help myself." A plan suddenly formulated in Tracey's head, and she turned to Ann, who recognized the look and backed up.

"Tracey? What are you thinking?"

"I really believe that if I don't give in and keep a distance between us for long enough, Derek will just get on with his life. Then eventually, if it's too much trouble, he'll see things my way and agree to the divorce."

"And how do you plan on doing this?"

"I need to disappear. In order to do that, I am going to need your help. Do you have your car keys with you?"

"Of course I have my keys, but how is that supposed to help you?"

"The plan is that I can take your car now and go find a hotel. Then after Derek goes home, have Dad take you and the boys home. When enough time has passed, I'll call you and bring you back your car. After that, I'll fly home, pack, and move."

"Tracey, what makes you think that Derek is going to give up that easy?"

"He's a smart man, and eventually, he'll come to realize that I am right. To try to make a marriage to a woman he doesn't love work is silly, and he'll let go. Please, Ann, give me your keys and then go downstairs and keep those two conspirators occupied so I can get away."

Ann reached inside her pocket and pulled her car keys off her key ring. As she reluctantly handed them over to her sister, she looked up to see Derek leaning with crossed arms against the doorjamb.

Tracey noticed her sister staring over her shoulder as she pressed the keys into her hand. Tracey closed her hands over the keys quietly, knowing immediately who must be standing behind her.

"Hi, Derek," Ann greeted him with false cheerfulness as Tracey tried to slip the keys into her pocket nonchalantly.

"Hello, Ann," he returned as he pushed himself upright. "Ann, I'd like a little alone time with my wife."

"No, Ann, please don't leave me alone with him," Tracey whispered frantically to her sister. Ann looked from one to the other, torn over loyalty to her sister and doing what she instinctively knew was right.

"Ann, have you ever heard of the expression 'tough love'?" Derek asked her.

"Ann, please," Tracey pleaded softly. Her tears began to spill over, nearly tearing Ann's heart out as she pulled away. "Sorry, little sister, but I promise I won't be far away."

As Ann passed Derek, she stopped and spoke quietly, "Hurt her, and you'll be dealing with me."

"Hurting her is not my intention."

"Your intentions notwithstanding, just don't." Then with a shake of her head, Ann left the room, hoping she had made the right decision.

Tracey brushed at the tears that kept sliding down her cheeks, trying desperately to stop them, as she did not want Derek to see her cry.

Derek gave her a few moments, hoping she would initiate the conversation. It didn't take long to realize that was not going to happen. Stepping up behind her, Derek placed his hands on her shoulders. "I have no intention of hurting you. We just need to talk."

Tracey shook her head and pulled away from his touch. She walked over to the rocking chair in the corner of her room; she sat down, still avoiding looking at him.

Kneeling beside her, Derek reached over and caught a tear on his thumb. "Please don't cry. We're going to work everything out," he told her as he pulled a tissue from the box beside her.

She pushed his hand away from her face. "I am not crying. I just got something in my eye."

Derek laughed softly at her returning spunk. "Honey, the only thing in your eye is your pride." Taking a tissue from the box beside her, he began wiping her face, resisting the urge to kiss her better. "Are you ready to talk to me now?"

Tracey grabbed the tissue from his hand and dashed away the tears from her face. "Apparently, I have no choice. So talk, get it over with, then get out."

"You are a stubborn woman."

"Since you realize that, why don't you give up now and save us both time and trouble?"

"Probably because like you, I have always liked a challenge, and you, my love, are definitely a challenge."

"I am not your love," she began. To herself, she added, *Unfortunately.*

"But you are my wife, and you might as well get used to the idea."

"I don't think so."

"You heard your father. There are not too many options open to us." He thought bringing in her father's logic would help his case. Wrong.

"My father, for some reason, does not seem to be thinking straight. I believe that if my father had this case come before him from any other couple, he would have found more options."

"It does not really matter to me if there are other options. I have decided on staying married to you. We stood in front of a minister and vowed to God to make this marriage work. Therefore, that is what we will do."

"Are you ordering me to stay married to you?"

"If that is what is comes down to."

"I have never taken orders very well in the past, and I don't think I'm likely to change my ways now."

"Then don't think of it as an order. Think of it as the right thing to do."

Silence.

"Tracey, you are always so logical and reasonable, so why are you making this so hard? We've known each other for over three years. We're a great team."

Silence.

"Tracey, I am willing to compromise on a year. If things have not worked out in that time, then I will give you your freedom."

Silence.

"Tracey, the papers have already gotten ahold of the fact that we are married. Do you want to face the press with a marriage that lasted three days? We'll end up on every tabloid paper across the country."

Silence.

"Look, now that we are married, the business is 50 percent yours. Negative publicity could ruin us."

"I don't want your business. It's yours."

"It's ours."

"No."

"Good Lord, you are a stubborn little witch." Derek got up and stood over by the window, trying to resist the urge to either shake her or kiss her into submission.

"Look, Tracey, this could go on all day. What will it take to make you see reason?"

"For you to go away."

Derek rolled his eyes and shook his head. "Okay, Tracey, the deal on the table is this. We live together for the next year. We give ourselves the chance to become friends, a chance to create a true relationship. The time will also give us a chance to see if we have any other repercussions from our wedding night. You wouldn't want to go through that alone, and if I helped create a child, I want to be a part of its life from the beginning."

"We could not have created anything the other night! Nothing happened!"

"You're not 100 percent sure of that, are you?"

Tracey shrugged. "Believe what you will. But the deal on the table is not acceptable."

"Too bad. It's your only choice."

"Not likely. All I have to do is wait you out. After a year, I file for divorce, and we're done."

"Only if I agree. Remember, my love, on irreconcilable differences, we *both* have to sign. All I have to do is tell the judge that I want reconciliation, that I don't think our marriage has had enough of a chance. I can and will keep it up forever."

"Are you telling me that if I don't give up a year of my life to you now, I'll be stuck with you forever?"

"I'm not sure if I like the phrasing, but that is the basic bottom line, yes."

She still thought her plan would work if she could just get him away from her, so she decided to change tactics.

"Okay."

Derek's eyes narrowed at her quick capitulation. He knew she was up to something, but he would play along. "Okay. Where's your suitcase? I'll help you pack."

"Uh, I can pack myself. Why don't you go on back to San Diego, and I'll follow up in a few days."

"No, I don't think so. Besides, I have already spent three days of my honeymoon without my wife. I don't plan on spending the rest of the week alone."

"Honeymoon?" She swallowed hard. "I really do not think that is necessary, and I don't think it is a required evil to a make-believe marriage."

Derek pulled Tracey to her feet and tipped her chin up so he could look into her face as he spoke. "A honeymoon was designed originally for two people to spend time away from others in order to get to one another better and to learn how to deal with one another on a different level. That is exactly what we need. In addition, this is no make-believe marriage. We are husband and wife, and we will act as such."

"I will not sleep with you."

"You will sleep in my bed beside me. Anything more than that, and you will have to be a willing and active participant. I have never forced a woman to do anything she didn't want to do before, and I don't plan on starting now, with my wife."

"A vow of celibacy? Wow, I am impressed."

"I never said I took a vow of celibacy. I just said I would not force you into anything."

"Well, since I do not plan on being a willing participant in anything, you are on the losing end."

"And what makes you think you won't?"

"Because this is a farce, and I am not going to get involved with you on any level. You can force me to be with you, but you cannot make me feel anything for you."

"Are you trying to tell me that you do not feel the chemistry between us?"

"There is no chemistry. It was just a drug of some sort."

"Want to bet?"

"What?"

"Want to bet that there is no chemistry? A chemistry that's been between us longer than Saturday night?" He raised an eyebrow at her. Then before she could argue, he asked, "Tell me you can't feel this." With that, he gently placed his lips on hers, actually giving her the opportunity to pull away. When she did not, he pulled her closer into his arms and deepened the kiss.

Tracey had meant to pull away the minute she realized his intentions, but like a moth drawn to the flame, she just stood there, mesmerized by him. His touch seemed to make her dizzy.

"As I said, it's chemistry." He said the words against her parted mouth.

When his words penetrated her fog-filled brain, they gave her the strength to move back a step. "So you're a good kisser. So was Danny, but I didn't sleep with him either." Danny had been the first love of her life—in the third grade.

"You didn't marry him either."

"I hate you."

"Would you like me to show you again that you don't?"

"Please leave me alone. I can't keep up with you today."

"Good, for once, I have the advantage. Somehow, I don't think that will happen too many times in our married life."

"Not if I can help it."

Before Derek could reply, a small body pushed itself between them. "Are you done kissin' my aunt Tracey? Are you really my uncle? Do you really have a ranch? Are we really invited?" Johnny rattled the questions off like a machine gun.

Derek gave Tracey a look to let her know he was not finished with her yet. With a shrug, Tracey moved away, leaving Derek to deal with her nephew. Derek squatted down in order to be on the same level as the child before answering all his questions.

"Hi, Johnny. No, I am not done kissing your aunt Tracey," he said as he glanced up at Tracey, smiling when he saw her stiffen. "But more can wait until later. I really am your uncle, and I could not be happier. Yes, I have a ranch, or rather, my family does, and yes, you are really invited. There, did I answer all your questions?" Derek smiled at the little boy, who grinned back.

"Wow, my mom always makes me go back and ask one at a time, but that just takes too long."

"Well, you must take after your aunt because she tends to ask questions just the way you do."

"Yes, she does, and we've been trying to break that habit since she was a kid without success, so it does not bode well for his father and I where this monkey is concerned," Ann spoke up from the doorway. Ann looked from Derek to Tracey, asking quietly, "Everything okay in here?"

"Just about as expected. Tracey is going to get her things packed so we can get started on our honeymoon. I have a reservation at one of the Victorian bed-and-breakfast hotels just outside of town."

"Well, I'm glad you two were able to work out an agreement," Ann said, but she was watching her sister, who was giving a small shake of her head and trying to communicate with her silently.

Derek watched the interchange and decided to let his new bride know just how much he already knew about her plans. "Oh, Ann, thank you for offering Tracey transportation"—he pulled the car keys out of his pocket and tossed them to his new sister-in-law—"but I rented a car, so she can go with me."

Shocked, Tracey put her hand on her jean pocket and found it flat with emptiness. How had he gotten them without her knowledge? How had he even known she had had them? She rolled her eyes in exasperation. He must have been standing in her doorway longer than either she or Ann had realized, which means he knew of her plans to leave him.

By this time, Johnny had enough of the adults ignoring him. "So, Uncle Derek, when can we come down to the ranch? Do you have horses to ride?"

"We raise horses on the ranch, so, yes, you can ride when you are down there. We have some very sturdy and safe mounts for you and your brothers. As for coming down, if it is okay with your mom, you can come down a week from Saturday for Aunt Tracey's and my wedding reception and stay as long as you want."

"Can we, Mommy, can we? Oh, please, we'll be good. I promise." Johnny ran to his mom.

"Of course we're going. Daddy is even off, so we can all go," she assured her son, but when she looked up from his shining face to Tracey's stormy one, she realized an explosion was about to happen.

"Johnny, why don't you go and tell your brothers about the trip?" When her son had left the battlefield, she turned to the combatants.

"It's okay, Ann. I think I forgot to mention the reception to Tracey. I think we may need a little more time together, alone."

"Uh, sure." She was at first hesitant, not knowing who to feel more sorry for—Tracey for the added pressure or Derek, who, if Tracey's face was any indication of her feelings, might not be long for this world. *Two peas in a pod*, was all she could think of at that point, and she began to back out of the room with a grin. "I'll be just down the hall. You know, just in case you need anything, such as a referee, first aid kit, or transfusion."

"Thanks, Ann, but I think I can handle her."

"Then you are a better man than most. I know that look. See ya." She laughed as she began to pull the door closed behind her adding facetiously, "Maybe."

"Great, more comedians added to the family tree," Derek spoke softly before turning around to face his wife. "Hi, honey, guess I left out a little information."

"No, what you did was cut off the limb that was holding you on to that family tree for the next year."

"And that means exactly what?" Derek asked softly as he began walking toward her.

Tracey backed away from him. "I am not going anywhere with you. I don't trust you. What else do you have up your sleeve? No, don't tell me. I don't want to hear anything more from you. I want you to leave."

"I leave only when you do. And talk about untrustworthiness. You were, in one breath, telling me that you were going to give our marriage a try, but all the time, you planned on ditching me and running off in your sister's car."

"That's different."

"Explain."

"Because I told you I didn't want to go, and you wouldn't listen. I figured if I left, you would understand that I was serious."

"Well, I am serious too. You either give this marriage an honest try for a year, or I will keep you tied to me forever."

"No!" she screamed at him. She picked up the nearest thing to her hand and threw it at him. He easily dodged the book and the cup, but the second book hit him in the chest before he could reach her. Capturing both of her hands in one of his, he gently tackled her to the bed. "Stop it."

"No." Tracey closed her eyes, deciding that ignoring him at this point would be best.

"Tracey, I know you're mad, but you need to listen."

"No."

"Tracey, the media knows we are married, and we want this to look as natural as possible, so I planned a reception for our family and friends."

"No."

"Tracey, if you just stop and think for a moment, you know what I am saying makes sense. Besides, I want to show off my beautiful new bride."

"No."

"Are you going to even hear me out? Give me a chance?"

"No."

"Okay, I guess we'll do this my way."

Tracey opened her eyes at that point, just in time to see his lips descending onto hers, and only had time for one breathless no.

She tried to move her head, but Derek held her captive, one hand still holding her hands and the other one now on her chin. He kept assaulting her senses by trailing slow, loving kisses along her neck and face, always returning to her lips. Her ability to ignore him and his touch was disappearing by the second, and she had no conscious idea when she stopped fighting and gave into her own natural feelings, kissing him back, reveling in his touch. When he let go of her hands, they went of their volition around his neck, cuddling him to her.

"So are you going with me?" he asked against her lips.

"No."

"Apparently, you need a little more persuasion." And this time, he let his hand trail down her side to find the hem of her shirt, sliding under and up until he could touch her soft skin. He felt her shiver.

"You know we have this chemistry between us, and we need the chance to explore it."

"No." The word was the same, but she was breathless, and it lacked conviction. They both knew it.

"Feel the magic, Tracey," he told her as he continued to run his hand over her rib cage, loving the feel of her. "Can you feel it, honey?"

"No." This time, she could barely get the words out.

"Little liar." He laughed gently as he nuzzled her neck. "Talk to me, Tracey?" he said. He could feel she needed to ask him something.

"Why? Why me?"

"Because for some reason, the fates put us together. The least we can do is find out why."

"I won't."

He kissed her again. "You will."

"I can't."

"You can."

"I don't want to."

He gathered her close in his arms. "Yes, you do." When she would have responded, he placed a finger against her lips. "Before you answer, I have no problem in continuing to show you how much you like my touch."

Tracey's head dropped to his chest in defeat. It was hard enough fighting him, but to have to fight herself as well was too much, for now.

"All right, you win. We'll leave here together."

Relief flooded through him as he rested his head on top of hers and continued to hold her close to his heart. He had one year to make her believe that this was where she wanted to stay, forever.

"Sid, old man that was a close call, but I think things are going to be okay now."

"Charlie, we both know these two hotheads, and okay is not something they will be for a while, at least until they don't have a time limit on themselves."

"But they both realize now that they belong together."

"Yeah, they each realize it for themselves, but they have yet to communicate that to each other."

"So what you are saying is that our wings aren't secure yet."

"That's exactly what I am saying."

"Okay. Any way we can help them?"

"At this stage? Stay on guard and pray."

4

"Would you like to stop for dinner before we get to the hotel?"

"No, thank you."

"Tracey, ever since we left your father's house, you have barely spoken a word. We have always been able to talk."

"I just don't have anything to say to you right now," Tracey told him as she continued to watch the sights of San Francisco through her window. He had been full of small talk since she had capitulated. He would since he had won, or so he thought.

She was quiet but cooperative as they checked into the hotel and oblivious to his thoughtful stares as he watched her.

At the door of their suite, he took great pleasure in swinging her up into his arms to carry her over the threshold. He forestalled her objection in front of the bellman by reminding her it was traditional. She narrowed her eyes at him but remained quiet,

Once he placed her on her feet in order to take care of the tip, Tracey began looking around, and for the moment, she forgot about her current problems because the room was breathtaking. It was like stepping back in time—from the early American fabric on the overstuffed couch, to the antique armoire that hid a modern television, video, and stereo system. In the back of the room next to a window that overlooked the San Francisco bay was a small antique dinning table with two high-back chairs. All around the suite, there were beautiful flower arrangements and candles set in crystal holders.

She could not resist walking around, touching the glass, running her hands over the silky wood, or smelling the flowers. "This is absolutely lovely."

"I agree," he said. He was not looking at the room, but at her.

When she knelt down by the ornate fireplace, she realized she could see through to the other side. Jumping to her feet, she ran to the double doors that separated the rooms. "Oh, look, a double fireplace!" she exclaimed. Derek lounged in the doorway, watching her with an indulgent smile on his face. It looked like he had finally managed to get at least one thing right with her, as well as having found another thing they had in common.

By this time, she had found the huge four-poster bed with its canopy of sheer drapes, and she was in awe. The intricate hand carvings on the bed's foot and headboards intrigued her. "This must have taken someone months to create. How did you ever find this place?"

"I happened to come across a brochure for this place. I love the stepping-back-in-time look and hoped you would too."

"I do. Thank you," she told him and then ran out of things to say.

The silence began to stretch, and Derek, afraid of going two steps back to the one step forward, made the next move.

"I have an idea. How about while I call for a light supper to be brought up, you unpack and get comfortable?"

"Uh, that would be nice. I could use a hot shower."

"They have a huge claw-foot tub in the bathroom. Why not try a long hot bubble bath?" he suggested as he left her suitcase on the bed within easy reach and closed the door behind him.

She was addicted to bubble baths. How could he have known that? "It's just a coincidence. You're getting a little paranoid," she chided herself.

Going over to her suitcase, she pulled out only what she would need for the evening. Then she locked the bedroom door before she put her suitcase in the closet.

Derek heard the click of the lock on the bedroom door, clearly telling him she didn't trust him. "I'll let you get away with that for tonight only, Tracey," he told the closed and now-locked door.

Tracey dawdled as long as she felt she could. Then after changing into her jeans and a comfortable tee shirt, she unlocked the bedroom door and stepped out. Then, not for the first time since all this had begun, Tracey wished this were real, for all around her was romance. A fire flickered in the fireplace, and candles lit the room while soft music played on the stereo.

"Dinner is served, madam." Derek held out her chair with an exaggerated bow.

"Thank you, kind sir." She smiled and played along, letting herself relax, telling herself to keep things light. Therefore, with that in mind, she let the playing continue and surprised herself by thoroughly enjoying their dinner.

Derek felt himself falling further under her spell as the evening wore on. She was playing, she was laughing, and he knew instinctively that as long as the conversation remained on anything but the future, she was his.

Dinner was long over when he decided to push his luck a little. Getting up from the table, he took her by the hand and into his arms to dance to the soft romantic music that had been flowing around them for several hours.

At first, she held herself stiff in his arms and chewed on her bottom lip; her heart and body were at war with her mind. Finally, giving into what she had been dreaming about all evening—being held in his arms—she gave a deep sigh and relaxed in his embrace.

Over the years, Derek learned to listen to music with his heart, but he had a feeling that Tracey listened with her head. Nevertheless, he hoped that she would listen to the words that were flowing around them now because to him, the song "I Swear" by Baker & Meyers was their song. He wanted to bring her attention to it, but something told him to leave it alone Therefore, he just pulled her closer and let the song tell her that he understood how scared she was and that he would do all in his power to make her never regret being with him.

For the next half hour, she was soft and pliant in his arms, her soft musky scent wrapped around him like a gentle blanket. Finally, he had to either step away or take the next step forward, taking the chance at losing her again. So reluctantly, he stepped back.

"You're exhausted, and since tomorrow is going to be a busy sightseeing and shopping day, why don't we get some sleep?"

Panic was her first reaction. She swallowed hard when Derek tipped her chin up and brushed a kiss across her lips softly. "Sleep, Tracey, nothing more, nothing less." He let her go then. "I'll go take a shower, which will give you time to get yourself settled." About a half hour in a cold shower should be enough to cool him off, he thought.

"Thank you," was all she could think to say at that moment.

"I'm not an ogre, you know."

"You don't want me answering that, do you?" She grinned at him.

He reached out and tweaked her nose playfully. "Careful, Tracey, I might start getting the impression you actually like me," he stated as he left the room, not waiting for a reply.

After she heard the bathroom door click shut, she answered that for herself, "It's not an impression. It's already a fact."

When Derek came out of the shower, Tracey was already in bed. She was lying under the blanket but on the sheet, and she was wearing her robe over her night clothes. With a sigh, Derek climbed into the bed, rolling over to her. She had her eyes closed and her back to him. She was controlling her breathing, as if asleep, but Derek knew better. He had told her she would sleep in his bed, and she was, so for now, he would leave it at that. He laid a gentle kiss on her temple. "Good night, Tracey. Sweet dreams." He rolled away onto his back, lying there quietly until he finally drifted off to sleep.

Tracey waited until Derek had been asleep for several hours. Hoping he was not a light sleeper, she slipped from the bed. Quietly, she slipped off the robe she had placed over her jeans and tee shirt. After leaving the robe balled up in her place on the bed, she tiptoed to the closet for her suitcase.

A tear escaped her eye as she stood by the bed for a moment and silently apologized. Then she went out of the bedroom to the door of the suite.

The door wouldn't budge. She tried and tried turning the lock this way at that. Then she spied the double-sided dead-bolt lock, one that required a key to get in or out. Where was the key? She searched everywhere. After twenty minutes, she knew it was nowhere to be found. She slid down the door in frustration and exhaustion. This was just too much for her, and the tears that had been starting and stopping for days began to flow uncontrollably, racking her body with sobs.

For an hour, Derek lay quietly, feeling her pain, but he knew enough to leave her alone. This was something she had to work out for herself. He had locked that security lock because something had told him she would try to make a run for it. Seversble, times while she cried so desperately, he almost gave up and handed her the keys he had kept with him all evening, but he could not let her go.

After two hours, he realized she would not come back to his bed willingly. If she had, he would have believed she was going to work with him. What he could not figure out was why she was willing to break her word; Tracey never broke a promise.

But did she actually promise to stay for the year, or did she just say she would go with you?

Why hadn't I thought of that? Tracey would never break her word. She had said the words I wanted to hear, but she never promised me a thing. Well, she will in the morning," he said to himself as he got out of the bed and went in search of his wife.

He knelt down beside her slumped form; she had cried herself to sleep. "Tracey, wake up, honey, and come to bed." He shook her gently but only got a murmured protest in response. "One way or another," he told her as he lifted her up into his arms.

Her head was resting on his chest when her eyes fluttered open. She then murmured sleepily, "I need to leave before you wake up." Her eyes closed again.

"Too late," he said as threw back both the sheet and the blanket before laying her down on the pillows. Then he removed her clothes before dressing her in one of his own tee shirts. "Nice try, and I'd say, 'Better luck next time,' but there is not going to be a next time."

After putting her clothes away, Derek climbed into bed beside her, pulled her into his arms, and fell asleep.

That was how Tracey woke the next morning, with a muscular arm holding her securely against him. The memory of the failed flight from the night before came flooding back; she even had a vague memory of Derek's carrying her back to bed.

Using two fingers, she tried to lift the heavy arm off her, but instead of removing the arm, it pulled out of her hand and tightened more securely around her. "Going somewhere?" The question came from behind her.

How could she answer that one? She couldn't, so she stayed silent. The bed creaked under Derek's shifting weight just before he pulled her over onto her back. "Good morning, Mrs. Callahan. Sleep well?"

"Well enough, I suppose."

"You know, I learned something new about you last night."

Silence,

"Aren't you curious?"

Silence,

"I found out you sleepwalk. Sometime during the night, you got up, got dressed, and even packed a suitcase. It was a good thing that I decided to lock the security lock. Otherwise you could have sleepwalked yourself right out of the room and into traffic."

Silence,

"Saved you twice in twenty-four hours. Don't I even get a thank-you for that?"

Silence,

"Not talking this morning?"

Silence,

"That's okay. I can think of other things to do besides talk." He started nibbling on her earlobe, his intention to keep nibbling clear.

"Okay, okay. Stop. I admit it. I tried to leave, you caught me, and I'm busted. Please let me up."

"Sure." He let her go, grinning as she jumped from the bed and realized she was only wearing her panties and his T-shirt.

"What? Where are my clothes?"

"You didn't expect me to put you to bed and have you be uncomfortable all night, did you?"

Tracey closed her eyes and prayed for strength. "Sorry, silly of me to think you would leave me any dignity or privacy," she snapped at him, stomping over to the closet, but her suitcase was not there. She went into the sitting room, also empty. She stormed back into the bedroom just in time to see Derek tucking his shirt into his jeans.

"Where are my clothes?"

"Where is my promise, your unbreakable word, to give this relationship a chance?"

"That's blackmail." So he'd figured her out.

"True. And your point would be?"

"That's illegal. You can't hold me hostage. People will wonder why I never leave this room."

Derek laughed. "Honey, we are on our honeymoon. Now think about what you just said."

"Oh, shut up."

"Your choice, honey, a promise for clothes, or I get to watch you running around in my T-shirt for the next year. And believe me, the view is not too bad from where I stand." Deliberately, he let his eyes roam down her shapely slender legs.

"All you are asking for is words. Who says that even if I say the words you want to hear, I won't leave the first chance I get?"

"Because you are too much like me. If you give someone your word or your promise, you do not go back on it. It's your bond, your reputation. It's why people know they can trust you. All I want is the simple words. 'Yes, Derek, I promise I will stay with you for the next year and try very hard to make this marriage a reality.'"

"Be reasonable."

"I'm trying. You are the one who is making this difficult. Say it, Tracey."

Silence.

"Okay, you think about it while I go and order us some breakfast."

Tracey stormed off into the bathroom, slamming the door behind her. By the time she had showered, she realized she had nothing clean to put on. She could put on the T-shirt, but all her personal clothing was in her suitcase. "This is not good."

So give in, she heard that voice in her head say.

If I do, I'm stuck with him for a year. No escape.

It's what you really want anyway.

He's only staying with me out of obligation and a perverse sense of humor.

You have a year to change that.

And if I can't, I walk away in a year with irreparable damage to my heart.

And if you walk away now, you still walk away with irreparable damage to your heart.

You're annoying.

Where do you think I learned it?

Shut up.

With a towel tucked securely around her, she left the bathroom and went to the sitting room door. "I promise to stay for the year and try to make our marriage look real."

Derek looked up from sofa, where he had been sitting and pretending to read a newspaper. "Excuse me?"

"I promise to stay for the stupid year."

"The wording leaves a lot to be desired."

"I promised. Now give me my clothes."

"Call me Derek."

"What?"

"You have never called me by name. Let's just call it the first step in fulfilling your promise."

"That was not in the deal for my clothes."

"So sue me." Derek got up and crossed the room, making her back up until she backed up into the bedroom and then into the bedpost, trapped.

"It's real easy, honey. Just say, 'Derek, can I have my clothes please?'" He ran the tip of his finger along the top of the towel, smiling as she shivered under his touch.

"Fine. Derek, can I have my clothes now?"

"Please," he reminded her as he dropped a kiss on her exposed shoulder.

"Please." The one word was full of meaning.

Taking temporary pity on her, he moved away. Going to the closet, he pulled out his suitcase and unlocked it. Reaching in, he pulled out her smaller case and placed it on the bed. "Here you go. Although I think of all the outfits I have seen you in, I like the one you have on now the best."

"Get out," she ordered, pointing to the door.

"But, Tracey," he teased her.

"Out!"

"Aww, you're no fun." He grinned at her. "Are you sure you don't need help?"

"Out," she said, but this time, an answering grin tugged at her lips.

"Okay, this time, but someday, you're going to find out that I can be a great help."

"Yeah, yeah. Someday, but for now..." She looked pointedly at the door.

"I know, I know—out."

To Tracey's relief, he left at that point, and she quickly changed into her only clean outfit. She had only packed for the weekend when she went to the wedding. When she had tried to tell him that they couldn't spend a week together, that she had to fly home in order to get more clothes, Derek had told her they would go shopping for clothing today.

"The man seems to have an answer to everything," she muttered to herself as she combed out the braid she had put in her hair the night before.

Then ask him the questions in your heart.

Oh no, then he'll know everything about me. That will give him way too much power, and he apparently has enough.

When did you get to be so stubborn?

Ask the heavenly Father. He made me this way.

She winced as she realized what she was doing again. *He must've also made me crazy, because I am beginning to talk to myself way too much these days.* She made short work of french braiding her hair and then left the bedroom.

"You look like a breath of spring," Derek complimented her as she stepped into the room. Her skirt swirled around her legs like a bouquet of blue and pink flowers on a cream-colored background. She had teamed it with a light blue sleeveless silk blouse. Her legs were bare down to the cream-colored sandals she had strapped to her slender ankles.

"Thank you," she answered softly, pleased that he liked the way she looked but suddenly feeling shy.

"How about indulging in a little nourishment before you drag me shopping?"

"Drag you?" she asked, lifting her eyebrows in question.

He held her chair for her, and then after she was seated, he answered, "Sure, you're the one who wants more clothes to wear. I was quite happy with the two outfits you were wearing this morning."

"Yeah, but you are the one that plans on dragging me sightseeing, and either one of those two outfits would get me arrested," she teased back.

"Hmmm, a compromise—you drag me, I drag you. Sounds fair. Or there is an alternative, you know."

Tracey looked up at him from spreading cream cheese on her bagel. "And that would be?"

"We could just stay in this room for the next week and get to really know one another. The room service is wonderful."

She gulped. "Eat. We have shopping to do."

The shopping trip was a success. The only fight they had was over who was going to pay. He insisted that the vacation was his idea, and therefore, he should. She said they were for her, so she should. They compromised. She would pay for anything she needed, and he would pay for anything he wanted her to have. She just never promised to wear them.

For the next week, they played like children, like friends. They wandered through the old military fort at the base of the bridge and took the boat tour around Alcatraz. In Chinatown, Tracey taught him how to eat with chopsticks, even though he complained throughout the meal that she was trying to starve him to death. During their stop at the fisherman's wharf, he fed her fresh steamed shrimp and made her sit still long enough for a sidewalk artist to create a pastel portrait of the two of them.

Everything was fine until the day before they were due to leave. It was their last sightseeing day, and they were in Ghirardelli square. They had just left the San Francisco House of Music, where they had bickered in fun over the purchase of a music box. "We do not need a music box. It could never compete over the music you already play constantly," she teased.

"Are you complaining? You don't like my singing?"

"Let's just say, don't quit your day job." She was only giving him a hard time because he had a wonderful, rich baritone voice that sent shivers up her spine every time he sang to her, which was quite often, as he either sang to her and or danced with her each night.

"You are a mean woman. I don't know why I put up with you."

"Anytime you say..." She left the sentence deliberately hanging.

"Oh, no, you're not getting rid of me that easy." He kissed the tip of her nose and then placed a hand at the small of her back to guide her to the next store. Unfortunately, the next store was a jewelry store.

"Hey, why don't we go in and pick out a real wedding set?" The words were out of his mouth before he thought about her possible reactions.

On the cloud above them, Sid and Charlie just cringed. "Oh no, here we go again."

While sitting in the backseat of the cab alone, Derek had time to reflect back on the jewelry store fiasco. All he had wanted to do was give her something more precious than the cheap gold bands they currently had. She'd gone ballistic.

A voice in his head chose that moment to chime in. *She's still having trouble with the entire idea of marriage, and you are trying to give her something very personal to marriage.*

She has a ring already. All I wanted to do was replace it, he defended himself silently.

But did you actually listen to what she was saying?

She was just being stubborn.

And you, of course, were being perfectly reasonable. Sid rolled his eyes in exasperation.

He flushed. *Well, I…I…okay, maybe not, but I've never known a woman who could get me so mad so fast before."*

Maybe because you care.

Of course I care.

Then next time, maybe you should listen.

Yeah, maybe I should. But did she have to run off like that?

She's a runner. You already knew that.

What if she's run off completely? What if she's not at the hotel when I get there?

She'll be there. She gave you her word. But how you handle it when you see her is going to be very important.

I know.

The taxi cab driver looked into his rearview mirror as he pulled up to the hotel and shook his head. This looked like one unhappy man.

"Sir, we're at your hotel."

Derek looked at the driver for a moment, uncomprehending, and then shook himself back to reality. "Sorry." He quickly paid off the driver, giving him a generous tip before making his way to his suite of rooms, hoping beyond hope that he had not scared his new bride completely out of his life.

He let himself into the suite quietly. When he saw the fire in the fireplace, he knew she was there. With a sigh of relief, he put down the packages he had in his hands and made his way to the bedroom. For a moment, he watched from the doorway at the beautiful picture she made. She was wearing a flowing white granny nightgown that she had bought; he knew she had made the purchase because she felt it was the least sexy bit of night wear she could find. However, that philosophy backfired because he felt it gave her an enchanting quality, and he found it extremely alluring, especially now, with her sitting on the floor in front of the fire, her hair flowing all around her as she combed out the damp tresses.

Tracey heard him come in and could feel his presence. She continued to comb her hair. The only evidence that gave away the fact that she knew he was there was that she began chewing nervously on her lower lip.

Without words, Derek moved and sat behind her, removing the brush from her hand and taking over the job himself. He was still brushing her hair long after it was dry. Not a word was spoken.

Finally, she reached up and placed her hand over his, stilling his movements. This time, she took the brush from his hands, putting it aside before leaning back against his chest. The silence continued for a while longer as they sat together, watching the fire dancing in the darkness.

"I'm sorry," she spoke so softly that he almost didn't hear her.

Derek lowered his cheek against the top of her head. "You have nothing to be sorry for. I was the one in the wrong this time. and I am sorry for upsetting you and ruining our day."

"Well, I should not have gotten so upset," she told him and then turned so she could look up at him. "I should have just gone in and picked out a trillion-dollar ring. You would have thought twice about it then." She grinned.

"You're incorrigible." He returned her smile before kissing her.

She snuggled down into his embrace, enjoying his touch and the fact that they had come through this problem without tearing each other apart.

Apparently, they had reached a new level; they had become friends.

～

"That was a close call."

"Sometimes, disagreements can make a relationship stronger."

"I think the expression is 'What doesn't kill us makes us stronger.'"

"Then these two are going to either kill one another or be the strongest couple in the world."

"Truer words were never spoken."

5

"You know, one of these days you are going to leave that glorious hair down," Derek told her as he watched her french braid her hair for their trip home.

"It gets in the way, but I haven't had the heart to actually cut it."

"I'm glad. Would you leave it down for me if I asked?"

"No."

"You're breaking my heart, you know, not even taking my feelings into account," he teased with a mock-sad expression on his face.

"I'm thinking you'll get over it."

"Heartless woman." He laughed and grabbed their suitcases. "Ready?"

"To face the world?" She made a face. "Not really, but somehow. I don't think that's going to get you to change your mind."

"No, but I'm thinking you'll get over it."

"Heartless man." She stuck her tongue out at him.

"See? The perfect couple."

Tracey just shook her head and headed out of the hotel suite and on to the beginning of their year of marriage. At least they had found friendly ground to walk on, or so she thought.

They had been on the road for a while when they stopped in Solvang, a little Dutch tourist town just outside Santa Barbara.

"I heard that they have a great fudge shop around here somewhere," Derek said with a grin.

"You have such a sweet tooth it is a wonder you are not a diabetic. You still have all that chocolate from Ghirardelli."

"Some of that is for the office. Besides, it's only a few flavors. And it's not fudge."

"It's nice to know you have a weakness."

"And you plan on using it how?"

"I'm not sure, but it may come in handy at some point." She grinned at him.

Derek loved this part of her. They had worked side by side for three years, and he had always seen her as a professional, serious but with a warm giving side. He had seen her laugh and play with their best friends, but never with him. With him, she had always been aloof. Even now, he knew she was still holding back with him, but he felt more hopeful now because of one silly little thing that meant a lot—she had learned to play with him.

When they got out of the car in Solvang, he reached for her hand to hold it as they walked through town. Except for a slight hesitation, she did not object. As they walked from store to store, he offered to buy her whatever she wanted, but other than a few souvenirs for their family and friends, she had not wanted to buy anything for herself. Then they came to a glass blower's shop.

Pulling him inside, she watched in fascination as the man behind the counter heated and twisted the long tubes of glass.

Derek stood back and watched her as she touched the finished pieces with reverence. When she lingered over a two-foot carousel, he knew he would buy it for her.

"No," she told him when he tried to make the purchase.

"Yes."

"No. It's a lovely piece, but no."

"Darn it, Tracey! Why won't you let me buy you anything?"

Tracey looked up at him but could hardly tell him the truth, because the truth was that anything he bought her would become a memory in which to mock her in a year, when she left.

"Okay, if you are so insistent, you can buy me that beautiful vase he is just finishing. But if you buy that for me, I get to buy you something," she told him reluctantly. As she watched the salesperson wrapping the beautiful vase, she made the decision that when she left, she would just have to leave it behind.

Happily, Derek paid for the vase, but then he had to accept her gift of five pounds of fudge. Life was looking good.

The expression "Too good to last" crossed his mind a short time later. They had come across a millinery shop. The window display had a beautiful wedding veil with a tiara headpiece made from opalescent crystals and porcelain roses.

"I know I made you an appointment with Christine for your dress, but I don't think she has anything like this in her shop. Would you like to go in and try it on? I think it will look beautiful on you."

"What are you talking about?"

"The wedding veil."

"Why would I want to wear a veil?"

"For our wedding and reception on Saturday."

"You mean the reception? I thought just a simple dress would be fine."

"You're the bride. You are supposed to look like one. Moreover, it's a wedding *and* a reception. Our families and friends were not with us for the first wedding, and we have no memories of it, so I thought I'd fix it and we could renew our vows in a small ceremony before the reception."

"Un-fix it."

"Be reasonable," he began and realized by her stormy face that that was probably the worst thing he could have said at the moment.

"Excuse me?" she began "You act in a high-handed manner—planning a wedding and reception without any thought as to my wishes and desires—and I am being unreasonable?" When her voice began to rise, she remembered they were in public and turned her back on him, making her way back to the car.

"Tracey, we need to talk this out."

She kept walking until she reached the car and waited for him to unlock the door.

"Tracey, we have come too far to go back now," he told her, but she only looked at the locked door and waited.

"Okay, have it your way and stay silent." He opened the door for her. Once he had gotten in and put the car in gear, he added, "Then I can talk uninterrupted until you can see reason." He looked at her clenched jaw and grimaced. Muttering to himself, he added, "And I have six hours to do it in."

Okay, maybe he needed more than six hours, he thought as he pulled into his driveway just under six hours later and looked over at the stubborn lady beside him. She still had not spoken a word.

"Okay, you may be mad at me, but Nellie has no idea that we aren't a couple in love, and I don't want her hurt. So I expect you to keep your promise and behave yourself."

Tracey shot him a scathing look as she climbed from the car. She reached the front door before he did but waited for him to join her. Then knowing what was coming next, she took a deep breath and made herself relax.

Derek scooped her up into his arms after opening the door, but when he would have made a comment, she placed a finger on his lips. "One word, and I will make you painfully sorry."

Deciding to accept her pliability, temporary as it would be, he left things alone, except for the stolen kiss he took before putting her down.

"Awe, young love, what a wonderful thing to see," Nellie said as she came into the foyer.

Tracey knew she was blushing, but she could do nothing about it when Derek made the introductions.

"I'm thinking this little girl is too good for the likes of you. How did you ever find someone so gentle and sweet?" Nellie teased the man before her.

"Hey, you've been around me since I was ten. How can you say something like that to me?" He pretended to be wounded.

"Because I've been around you since you were ten," Nellie returned with a laugh.

"Wonderful. Somehow, I think I am outnumbered and possibly in trouble."

"Hardly outnumbered. You have Barney," Tracey reminded him. And as if hearing his name, Barney came barreling down the hallway.

"Sit." The quick quiet command had Barney skidding to a stop to sit at Derek's feet.

"He's missed you and your runs down the beach," Nellie told him. "I'm okay for an occasional walk, but these old bones don't run for no one."

"I'd say I missed running too, but this one not only keeps me on my toes, she keeps me running," he teased and pulled Tracey to his side. He could feel her resistance but knew she would not make a scene. "But, Barney old' boy, I'll take you for a nice long run right after I show Tracey up to our room."

"That's okay. Go ahead and take the dog. I'll just keep Nellie company and get to know her a little bit better." She tried to pull away; she wanted to do anything that would postpone not only being alone with him, but alone in his room—his domain.

"That's okay, honey. We'll have plenty of time for visiting. I know you must be tired from your long drive. I'll tell you what, you go on upstairs and maybe have a nice relaxing bath, and I'll fix you a cup of hot herb tea and bring it up to you, Nellie offered.

When Tracey would have protested, Derek stepped in, "Thank you, Nellie that would be wonderful." Bending down, he ruffled Barney's furry neck. "Be back in a second, you hairy little hound." Then as he stood up, his arm captured Tracey around the waist, guiding her toward the stairs.

"I can walk on my own," she ground out from between clenched teeth.

"I know, but I enjoy touching you."

"You enjoy making me mad."

"That too."

Tracey just rolled her eyes, giving up for now.

Derek showed her around the upstairs of his big beachfront house. He had had three spare bedrooms all professionally decorated. They each had their own bathroom for privacy. At the end of the hall, she saw a set of double doors and knew that was Derek's room. When she would have bolted, he tightened his hold around her waist. "Oh no you don't, you gave up your running shoes, remember?"

"I thought I could do this, but I've changed my mind."

"Tracey, nothing has changed. We've been sharing a room for a week now. Besides, the only difference between walking into that room and this one is the fact that we are friends now."

"We are not," she told him as he literally pulled her into his room.

"What do you mean by that?"

She looked at him coldly. "Friends don't lie to friends."

"When have I ever lied to you?"

"You lied by omission. And I will not be a participant to further lies. I will not go through a phony marriage ceremony."

"There is nothing phony about our marriage, but we have nothing to show for it."

"We have a marriage license, and we'll have a divorce decree. What more could we ask for?"

"Is that all you want to show our child?"

"There is no child. How many times do I have to say that?"

"We do not know that for sure, and I, for one, do not want to tell my son or daughter that they were an accident. Most couples have pictures to display. We *will* have pictures."

"This is a useless argument because it is *not* going to happen."

"It will."

"No, I don't think so."

"It will, even if I have to carry you there kicking and screaming."

"Oh, and that will look just wonderful. How will you explain that to our friends?"

"I'll just tell them you were upset over having to leave our bed."

"You wouldn't dare."

"Try me."

"I will not wear a wedding gown."

"You will look like a bride, even if I have to dress you myself. I mentioned before that I made an appointment for tomorrow with a family friend, Christine. She owns CC's Gowns. She'll help you find something appropriate."

"And if I don't go to this appointment?"

"Then I will go and pick something out for you. I shopped enough with you in San Francisco to know your size and your style," he informed her as he pulled his running clothes from a drawer and began changing.

Tracey turned her back on him, cringing as she heard him laugh softly. "I sleep next to you every night with nothing on, and yet you panic every time you see me change clothes. Why?"

"I don't panic. I just don't want to watch."

Derek placed his hands on her shoulders and kissed the back of her neck "Liar," he whispered in her ear, and then before she could respond, he left the room.

After Derek had left, Tracey wondered around, admiring the fact that the room looked like an extension of the ocean view, which she could see out the glass doors and windows that led to a balcony that ran the length of the room. Above the fireplace was a huge oil painting of the incoming tide at sunset. Brass and glass sconces were on either side of the picture; each held soft-blue tapered candles.

Two high-backed chairs flanked the fireplace, with an antique oak table between them. Tracey gently touched the statuary of the dolphins frolicking in the waves that rested on the table.

The bed was a huge four-poster oak bed with a soft seafoam-green quilt. A jumble of matching green and blue pillows were piled at the head of the bed. Brass and glass lamps were on each side of the bed

Pictures of ships and maps were hung around the room, and an oak display case held antique pirate swords. "Oh my, no wonder I have such a hard time winning against the man. I think I married a pirate."

An hour later, she stood on the balcony, sipping tea and watching the sun set over the ocean, wishing all of this was real.

"Dear Lord, help me. Help me find a way to stop this before everyone involved gets hurt." She spoke softly.

The truth never hurt anyone.

The truth is that I love him, but he does not love me.

Are you sure?

I'm very sure. Up to two weeks ago, I was just his employee or just the best friend of his best friend's girlfriend, Tracey said to justify her feelings.

You have a year to get him to think of you differently, a year in which to get him to fall in love with you, if he hasn't already.

He's not, and I'm afraid.

Of?

Of failing and letting him and everyone else down.

You're afraid for yourself.

Yes, she breathed out the agreement and closed her eyes. *Yes, God, I am afraid for myself—afraid I don't have the strength to see this through, afraid he will never love me as I love him.*

Then pray for the strength.

But what am I praying for strength for? Strength to wait? Or the strength to survive the broken heart?

Strength to stay true to your faith in God and in the fact that he knows what is best for you and the strength to know that if you give yourself over to him, he will lead you in the right direction.

She watched Derek run back toward the house from down the beach. Tears slipped slowly and unnoticed down her cheeks as she wished that she were here under any other circumstances. She wished for this to be anything but what it was—a fake marriage with a one-sided love. So she wished for love and prayed for strength.

Derek settled Barney for the night and then made his way up to the room. He'd seen her on the balcony as he jogged up the beach. He knew she was crying and wanted to go to her, but instinct told him she needed this time alone. So he headed instead for the shower, but like the jog down the beach, the shower was doing nothing to get his need for her off his mind. In fact, it was worse because the musky scent of her shower gel still lingered in the steamy air.

"Okay, Lord, you are making patience a hard thing to achieve," he ground out as his desire for the woman outside became palpable.

She's not ready for you in that way.

I know. So could you give me a break once in a while? No matter what I do or where I go I see her, I feel her, and I smell her. I need her.

You need her to be ready for you, or you will lose her forever. Sid reminded him.

I know, but patience has never exactly been one of my finer qualities.

That's an understatement. Stay strong.

The mind is willing. It's the flesh that is weak.

Find the strength.

Reaching out, Derek turned the hot water off and let the shock of cold water hit his body "Lord, save me from pneumonia." But as his body cooled, his mind cleared, and the strength in his resolve returned.

Once showered and changed, he joined Tracey out on the balcony. Sliding up behind her, he placed his arms around her and nuzzled her neck. "Still mad at me?"

"Yes."

"Going to go to the appointment with Christine tomorrow?"

"Do I have a choice?"

"You always have a choice."

"What a choice. Either I go, or you do. That's not fair."

"Never said it was fair. I only said it was a choice."

"I'll go."

"Good, I promise it won't hurt," he teased her, hoping for a smile.

No smile was forthcoming, just the feel of a tear dropping onto the arm encircling her waist. Tightening his arm, he pulled her back against his chest, and he just held her as they watched the sun set on their first night home.

"Why couldn't he give in on this one?"

"Getting married again means to him that the vows are said with conscious thought. This makes it a vivid memory of making a memorable promise before God and their family, makes the marriage a reality. And with their strong beliefs in the Lord and his word, a marriage that feels more real will be harder to give up on. She's not able to be a wife to him and give her love to him because she doesn't 'feel' married. He wants to give that to her."

"You're right, and he is making a good move because somewhere along the road, her faith has begun to slip, and I've been unsure how to help her. Maybe this will be the solution."

"Well, his heart is in the right spot, but the way he is getting there is leaving a lot to be desired."

"But they wouldn't be who they are if they took the easy way to the right road."

"True, very true. I wonder in which direction the next road will take them."

"Don't ask because I don't think we want to know the answer just yet."

"Coward."

"That's me."

By the time Tracey awoke in the morning, Derek was
gone leaving her a note stating he was going to go into
the office to check on things while she went in for her
fitting. The note went on to say that he would have her
car brought to the house for her. This did not improve
her disposition. Apparently, while he played the working
man, she was expected to play the housewife with nothing better to do than shop.

The next few hours did nothing to improve her current disposition, so Tracey arrived at Christine's impatient and with a poor attitude. Christine had known
the Callahan men for most of her life and was quite use
to their overbearing ways, so she quickly understood
Tracey's mood. It was not long before the two women to
became fast friends, which soon brightened Tracey's day
and disposition.

"That one is just beautiful on you," Christine complimented a while later as Tracey tried on the sixth gown.

Tracey stood on the dressing platform, mirrors sur-
rounding her, and gave a sigh. "It is beautiful, just like the
others, but it's just that..." She trailed off. The gown was
a dream gown, with its crystals and lace on a background
of cream silk.

"What's the matter, Tracey?"

Tracey stepped down off the platform and sat down
with a sigh. "I don't know. These gowns are every woman's dream."

"But?" Christy looked down at her new friend.

"I don't know. It seems to be missing something. Just like the others."

"I don't think the dresses are missing something. I think you are."

"You know, Christy, you may be right, but the man says I either find something to wear or he will, and frankly, I…" Tracey trailed off as her eyes spotted the perfect dress.

Christy turned to look at what had caught Tracey's eye. She closed her eyes in silent prayer. "Tracey, you wouldn't."

"It's perfect."

"You couldn't."

"Oh, I would, and I could, and"—she paused for a moment in thought—"I think I will."

"Derek will have a stroke, or if he doesn't stroke out, he'll kill you and probably me."

"It was his idea."

"Tracey, I don't think that dress is his idea."

"He said, 'Go to Christine's and pick out a dress from her shop.' So I am picking out a dress in your shop." Tracey smiled at her new friend. "Don't worry, I won't let him touch you."

"What was God thinking when he put you two together?"

"I think he was having a bad day. I'm just trying to help him rectify it. So will you help me out of this gorgeous dress and save it for a more worthy bride? Then let's get my dress ready. Will you bring it to the ranch Saturday morning? I wouldn't want Derek to see it before the wedding. It's bad luck, you know."

"It's going to be bad luck no matter when he sees it."

"Well, I want to surprise him."

"That, Tracey my friend, is a guarantee."

"Good, then I'll get my point across." Tracey laughed delightedly as she went back into the dressing room to change back into her street clothes.

Christy went to the dress rack and pulled out Tracey's size. "Tracey, don't you want to try the dress on to see how it fits?"

"No, I know it'll be perfect."

"But seeing how this may be the last dress you ever wear here on earth, shouldn't you be very sure?"

Tracey came out of the dressing room, pulling her credit card from her purse.

"I'm very sure, so sure that I don't even care about how much it costs."

"Put your money away. Derek already gave me his visa number to charge whatever you wanted."

"Oh, no, maybe under other circumstances that would be okay, but this time, this dress is on me."

"Great, I meet the woman for the first time, and she signs my death warrant not only once but twice."

"Oh, Christy, believe me, by the time the bill comes in with today's date on it, and the dress isn't on the charge slip, I don't think he'll even notice. But if he asks, I'll tell him I made you. He'll believe that."

"I take back what I said before. Now I know why God put you two together."

"And that reason would be?"

"In order to keep two stubborn, pigheaded people from endangering two other innocent lives."

Tracey signed the charge slip with a grin. "If you weren't so intrigued with the idea of getting even with

Derek for tormenting you off and on over the years, you would have just refused to sell me the dress."

Christine laughed then; she had to agree that watching Derek get his for once was going to be fun. "Well, not too many people would be able to get away with this, you know."

"I know, but I have a guardian angel that keeps a pretty close eye on me, so I'm not afraid," she told her new friend as she hugged her before leaving and adding to herself, "Not too afraid anyway."

"And how am I supposed to get her out of this one?"

"I don't know. I'm having enough trouble keeping him in line."

"We are in so much trouble."

6

Unfortunately, the day she had been dreading all week had dawned bright and clear. *A beautiful day for a wedding,* Tracey thought as she looked out the window and watched the preparations for the reception being completed by the caterers that Derek had hired. "Too bad it is the right thing for all the wrong reasons." She sighed.

"Are you about ready to go and get dressed?" Robert asked his daughter as he walked into the room. "Your sister is waiting upstairs to help."

"I'll never be ready for this, Dad. I can't believe you are not only going along with this but that you are actually encouraging it."

"Tracey, I prayed for the strength to guide you in the right direction. Have you prayed?"

"Of course I prayed."

"You prayed, but did you listen for the answer?"

"I have to go get dressed now." Tracey avoided the question because she was not sure of herself or her faith at the moment.

"Someday, you are going to have to stop running. Because no matter how far you run or how fast you go, God is there, waiting for you to pay attention."

Tracey reached up and kissed her father's cheek. "I know you mean well, but faith and prayers have not worked for me this time."

"Why would you say that?"

"Because I asked for this day not to arrive, and it did." With that said, she left the room.

Robert closed his eyes and offered up a prayer for his lost child. When he opened them, Derek was in the room. "I'm sorry, I didn't mean to disturb you," Derek said as he entered the room.

"You didn't disturb me, son. How are you holding up?"

"I'm okay." He looked at his father-in-law and smiled. "I think."

"Spoken like a true bridegroom."

"I shouldn't be. We've been married for two weeks now."

"You may have been married on paper for two weeks, but this is actually going to be your true wedding day, and the real start to your marriage will begin today in every way," Robert said meaningfully.

"How did you know that?" Derek asked in surprise.

"I trusted you to go slow, to give you both the time you needed to get to know one another better. I also trusted you not to do anything she wasn't ready to accept. I had faith in you, or I would never have trusted you with my youngest child. Besides, as nervous as you both are today, I knew my trust had not been in vain."

"We haven't exactly found our feet yet."

"I know. She told me you blackmailed her into being cooperative."

"She told you?"

"Sure, she thought I would get mad and make you cancel everything."

"Why aren't you?"

"Because you are the man that God chose for her."

"What makes you so sure?"

Robert looked at his nervous son-in-law for a moment before answering him. "She spent the night here last night. Did you miss her? And before you answer, you might want to look at your tired eyes in the mirror."

"Of course I missed her. She's the type of woman who very quickly gets under one's skin."

"If you were not the man for her and, in turn, her for you, then you would not have missed her. In fact, you would have relished in the freedom. Believe me, you two were meant for one another, and I know she does care for you. Things are just going to take a little time to smooth out."

Robert would reassess those words an hour later when the bishop was in the study, waiting for the young couple to come before him. It was time to begin the ceremony. Robert left Derek at the bottom of the stairs while he went up to knock on the bedroom door where Tracey and her sister would be waiting. When the door opened, Robert looked nervously from his daughter to the man waiting in the black tux below. "Tracey, please tell me you are not going to do this?"

"Excuse me, I do not want to be in the middle of this," Ann stated as she left the room as quickly as she could.

"Don't you like the dress that Derek made me buy? I'm sure Derek will," Tracey stated as she moved past her father and stepped out of the room.

Derek looked up at the sound of her voice, expecting to see a vision in white. What he saw was a vision in black—not even a formal black gown, but a black silk suit. Her hair was scraped back into a tight bun at the back of her neck. She looked like she was going to a funeral.

"Tracey!" The anger in his voice made more than the one word unnecessary.

"What's the matter? Don't you like my dress? You asked me to go to Christine's and pick something appropriate out, and I couldn't find anything more appropriate than this."

"Tracey, you have one minute to go and change."

"Or you'll do what? Sorry, the only other thing I have to wear is a pair of jeans. They are definitely more comfortable than this. Should I wear those?"

"I swear—"

"Swearing in front of the bishop? How sacrilegious of you. Well, I guess if this is unacceptable to you, we'll just call the whole thing off." She shrugged, acting a lot more confident than she actually felt.

Adam grabbed Derek's arm to keep him from charging up the stairs; at the same time, Robert pushed Tracey back into the room.

"Let me go, Adam. I have a wife to strangle."

"Homicide is a capital offense."

"Not if it is justifiable."

"Derek, even you have to admit that she gives as good as she gets from you."

"Let me go, Adam," Derek demanded.

"Let her father talk to her."

Derek didn't want to, but he left her to her father while he paced the hallway like an angry caged tiger. The next fifteen minutes began to feel more like fifteen hours.

While Derek paced downstairs, Robert paced angrily upstairs.

"Tracey, I raised you better than this."

"You raised me to be independent."

"I have never seen anyone so angry before."

"You haven't been around me this week. Dad, he actually ordered me to buy a dress, threatening to pick one out and dress me in it if I didn't. So I did."

"You are not following your heart. You are just being spiteful. It's a good thing that your sister thought to bring down your mother's wedding gown. She wore it. Now you can too."

"Please, Dad, not Mom's gown. It's a special gown and was worn both times with love. Mom and Ann said vows in that gown, vows that meant something to them both. I will not wear it in a ceremony that has no meaning." Tracey went to stand by the window, trying to hide her tears.

"Tracey, do you love this man?"

Tracey closed her eyes, knowing she could not lie to her father, so after a long pause, she answered honestly, "With all my heart."

"Then tell him."

"I can't. He's already staying with me out of a warped sense of obligation. I don't want him staying with me longer because he feels trapped."

"Then show him how much you care and give him a chance to fall in love with you."

"How do I do that, Dad?" She turned to her father, who by now had lain her mother's wedding gown on the bed and was in the process of laying the veil next to it.

"Pray." Robert hugged his child to him one more time. "Pray for guidance, and this time, listen with an open heart." He kissed her cheek and left the room.

Crossing the room, Tracey gently touched the heavy satin of her mother's wedding dress. The once-white gown had aged to a soft ivory. The heart-shaped bodice sparkled with crystal beading, the same beading that was sewn into floral clusters scattered sparingly over the skirt. The sheer long sleeves ended in beaded cuffs. This dress had been made to make a bride's love shine.

Dropping to her knees, she first talked to her mother. "I wish you were here with me now. Dad tries, but I know you would understand. Please tell me what do to. I need your help and guidance." Her head dropped into her hands, and she prayed. She prayed to her mother and her heavenly Father for guidance, for answers, for knowing which direction was right.

Eventually, she climbed to her feet, and just when she thought the good Lord had forsaken her, she looked up and saw herself in the mirror. She saw a sad woman wearing funeral black. Then her eyes were drawn to an object on the bed, and she slowly turned around to look closer. Her mother's veil and headpiece were identical to the one that Derek had wanted so badly for her to try on when they were in Solvang. How coincidental was that? "Oh, heavenly Father, what are you trying to tell me?"

Downstairs, Robert joined Derek as he paced. "Give her time. Have faith."

"I'm trying." Derek looked up the empty stairs to the closed door at the head of them. "I'm trying."

After another quarter of an hour, Robert sent Ann to check on her sister. Ann disappeared into the room, and for another half hour, the men waited.

The sound of a door opening had both men looking up, and they knew the wait had definitely been worth it.

Tracey now stood at the top of the stairs, the beautiful wedding gown flowing around her. Ann had helped her curl her hair, using the crystal-and-porcelain tiara to pull the sides away from her face. They had left the long tresses flowing down her back, just the way Derek wanted to see it.

Ann stepped around her sister, stopping only long enough to squeeze her sister's hand and kiss her cheek. "Ann, wait," Tracey whispered as she began to panic.

"No, Tracey. It's all up to you now." Ann pulled her hand free, then turned and went down the stairs, stopping her father as he would have gone up to escort his daughter down. "No, Dad, not this time. This time, she has to do this on her own. She has to take the first step."

Robert looked from one daughter to the other and realized what Ann was trying to tell him. Tracey had made a move, but she had not yet made the commitment. With a nod, he let Ann know he understood.

Tracey watched her father step away from the stairs and felt abandoned. Chewing lightly on the inside of her lip, she turned and finally looked at Derek. Was he still mad? Was she doing the right thing? If she went through with this, would she be trapping them both into a loveless marriage? A step back was safe, was a step forward the same?

Derek could feel her indecision and watched her carefully, and he was afraid she would bolt at any second. He stepped forward to go to her. However, just as Ann had done to him, Robert put his hand on Derek's arm, stopping him. "No, Derek, she needs to do this on her own," Robert spoke in a whisper.

"She needs help," Derek answered his father-in-law, but his eyes never left Tracey's.

"She needs to have faith. She needs to make a commitment."

Time seem to hang in suspension as the bride stayed poised at the top of the stairs and the groom reluctantly stayed at the bottom. Neither moving until Tracey's eyes broke contact to look back to the safety of the room behind her. However, before she could move in that direction, a movement below caught her attention, and she turned back to see that Derek had reached out a hand, palm up toward her.

Looking around, she saw her sister, Ann, standing with her husband Ron and their three sons. Derek's brother, Adam, was there, holding his baby girl, Amanda. The youngest brother, Jon, stood behind their family friend and her new friend, Christine. Behind the bishop was Rick and Susan, the friends whose wedding they had gone to Vegas for. As her eyes fell on her father, she saw his love shinning from his eyes even before she saw him place his hand over his heart.

Then there was Derek, who stood just below her, looking so handsome, so strong, and so confident that this was the right thing to do. These people were her family, her friends, and her future.

Tracey looked back once again to the sanctuary of the room and made her decision; slowly, she descended the stairs until she could reach out and place her hand in his.

Derek closed his hand around hers and gently pulled her forward until she was on a stair that had her on face level with him. With the one hand still holding tight to hers, he lifted his other one to touch her face and then cup her chin. "You are so beautiful."

"Thank you."

"No," he told her gently as he brushed a featherlight kiss on her lips and then rested his forehead against hers. before adding, "Thank you."

Love just glowed around the couple on the stairs, so much so that there was not a dry eye in the crowd—at least until the bishop spoke, "Excuse me, but the kiss comes after the ceremony. The Lord and I would appreciate it if you two would stop rewriting his script."

Derek turned around as Tracey went down another step, still holding tight to Derek's hand. "Then he should have blessed us with more patience than he did," was Derek's honest reply to the minister as he winked at Tracey.

"Well, since you two are so impatient and we are all gathered here, we might as well begin."

So standing there right on the stairs, the bishop began the ceremony. No one was praying harder than Derek when the bishop asked Tracey if she would take Derek as her lawfully wedded husband, and no one felt more relief than he did when he heard her whispered "I do."

After the ceremony, everyone wanted time with the couple. However, finally after an hour, Derek was able to pull his lovely bride into his arms as they began the first dance together. Everyone watched the two of them from the sidelines, but Derek and Tracey only had eyes for one another.

"Are you still mad at me?" Tracey asked him, worried that when he got her alone, he would still probably kill her.

"I should be," he told her, trying to sound tough without succeeding.

Knowing from his tone that she was safe, she ran her hand down the lapel of his black tuxedo and teased him, "But I thought you liked black."

"You thought I'd have a heart attack."

"You should have seen your face. I think I darn near succeeded." She laughed up at him.

"Brat, maybe I should beat you once a day just for general purposes." He pulled her closer to him until she rested her head against his chest.

Turning her head, she looked up at him. The teasing went out of her eyes, and her hand reached up to touch his cheek. "I am sorry, you know."

"I know. So am I." He turned his head and kissed the palm of her hand, sending a shiver of warmth through her. Tracey cuddled closer until she could hear his heartbeat. A heart that she hoped would someday belong to her.

When the music ended, Derek reluctantly turned her over to her father for the next dance. Then for the next few hours, the young couple talked, danced, and socialized with their guests, but their glances were never very far from one another.

"Happy?" Robert asked his daughter later in the evening.

"Dad, to tell you the truth, I am not sure what I feel, other than I am still unsure of what the future will bring."

"Then maybe you need to concentrate on the here and now. Give your fears to the Lord and let him guide you to your future."

"That is so much easier said than done."

"Nothing worth having is usually ever easy."

"Sorry to interrupt," Derek said as he approached father and daughter, although he looked anything but sorry as he snaked an arm around Tracey's waist. "Come dance with me."

When Tracey would have objected, her dad waved her away. "Go and dance," he told her, but stopped her a moment later. "Tracey?"

"Yes, Dad?"

"Promise me?"

Tracey looked from one man of her heart to the other. "I can only promise to try."

"That's all I'm asking."

Out on the makeshift dance floor, Derek swung her into his arms. "And just what are you promising your father?"

"That is none of your business." *Oh, good, Tracey, that was a great start to keeping that promise*, she thought.

"I think I stayed away too long. You're getting all prickly again. Maybe I should make up for that."

"And how do you propose to do that?" she asked, swallowing her nervousness.

"By keeping you closer to me from now on." With that said, he pulled her closer to him, slowing his steps and letting the music swirl around them.

Tracey let herself become lost in the warmth of his arms and the masculine scent of his cologne, so lost that it took a few minutes to realize the warm kisses being placed on her temple and eyes were not apart of her dream but a reality.

"I missed you last night," he told her as he brushed another kiss across the top of her head. "Miss me?"

"I'd rather not say. It might incriminate me." She smiled up at him, giving him the opportunity to drop a kiss on her lips.

"You didn't miss that last night? Or cuddles and hugs?" he asked as he hugged her tightly to punctuate his words.

"Maybe a little." *Or maybe a lot*, she added to herself.

"Feeling like a bride yet?"

"In this outfit? I'd better," she teased.

"Tracey, I..." How did someone ask his wife if she was ready to be his wife? "What I mean is..."

Tracey's eyes narrowed in curious puzzlement. "What is it? I've never known you to have trouble talking before."

"I just don't want to scare you or make you feel like I'm pressuring you because you know I'll wait for as long as it takes, but..."

"What are you talking about?"

"Tracey, every relationship has levels, and in order to grow, you go from one to the next when it's right. And I know up to now that you didn't really feel married, but now, I was hoping...oh, never mind." He sputtered to a stop, tucked her head under his chin, and kept swaying to the music.

Tracey stayed quiet in his arms, letting his words actually penetrate her fog-filled mind. When realization hit, she was surprised she didn't have the sudden urge to run. In fact, a warm feeling surrounded her heart.

Letting instinct guide her, she tipped her head up as she smiled up at Derek, making him catch his breath for a second time that day. Sliding her hand up around his neck, she pulled him down to her. "Are you asking me if I am ready for more of things like this?" She kissed him then, the first kiss she had ever initiated. After a few moments, she made herself pull back, and she placed her hands on either side of his face. "If that is the question on the table, then the answer is yes."

"You pack one heck of a punch, lady." His breathlessness gave her no doubt that, although he may not love her, he did indeed want her, and that gave her hope that love just might grow.

"Want to fight some more?" she flirted with him, feeling pure feminine power for the first time in her life and loving it.

"You fight like that any more here in public, and someone's going to have us arrested." He kissed her hard and fast before swinging her up into his arms, making her squeal. "I think it is time for us to leave this shindig and go home."

"I should be mad over this high-handed manner of yours," she told him as he carried her off the dance floor.

"And are you going to get mad?" he asked, but he didn't appear overly worried about her answer.

Ignoring the cheers, laughter, and soft soap bubbles that were floating down all around them, she wound her arms around his neck and nipped lightly on his earlobe. "Maybe later," she said as she trailed kisses down his neck to his collarbone.

"Stop that, you little witch, or we'll never make back to the house," he growled at her. Her only response was to give a laugh of pure evil femininity.

"Wave good-bye to our family and friends, dear, for you may never see them again," he told her as began to lower her into the back of the waiting limousine.

Once the car pulled away, Derek closed the window between the driver and the back before returning to his bride. He wanted to ask what had changed her mind about being with him, but he was afraid to spoil the moment. So he just kept her in his embrace, cuddling and kissing her enough to keep her with him, but keeping a tight rein on his feelings in order not to scare her.

Once they arrived at back at the beach house, he sent the driver on home and again carried his bride over the threshold. Tracey was more than willing this time and stayed with him, kiss for kiss and touch for touch, until they had actually reached the bedroom.

Once in the room, he placed her on her feet, kissing her one more time before stepping back to remove his tuxedo jacket.

As the cool air touched her, she was forced back into reality. Tracey began to watch him with eyes that had begun to show her uncertainty. When she realized just what level she had wanted to be moved to, she stepped back in a moment of fear.

"Oh no, Tracey, don't retreat on me now." Derek reached out and pulled her back into his arms.

"I'm sorry, but I don't think—"

"Tracey, for once, don't think. Feel." He ran the back of his knuckles down her cheek, gently before cupping the back of her head, his thumb still moving gently on her skin. He kissed her slowly and softly. "Just feel the magic."

"I want to, but—"

"Then let yourself, but always know you can trust me to stop. No one should ever feel forced into making love. We will only go as far as you want to go, okay?"

"Okay," she answered him softly.

"So what do you want?" he asked, giving her the chance to change her mind.

What did she want? she asked herself. As she wrapped her arms around his neck, she offered up her lips for a kiss and answered him honestly, "You."

"I believe I can accommodate that." And he did. For the rest of the night, he gave himself to her, fitting himself to her needs and desires.

Therefore, it was with gentle love that the groom finally took his bride and their relationship to the next level—husband and wife.

"Success!" Charlie sat back on his cloud happily.

"It was close there for a while. I thought for sure she was going to bolt before the wedding."

"Either that or he was going to give up the fight and let her go."

"Well, neither happened, thanks to Him." Sid reminded Charlie.

"Thanks to their renewed faith in Him." Charlie corrected him

"I think this situation calls for a little vacation," Sid said as he rubbed his hands together with glee.

"What makes you think this is over?"

"It's not?"

"Not until we get them past the one-year mark, the deadline they gave one another."

"This is going to be a long year for us."

"Equivalent to a lifetime." Charlie replied with a deep sigh.

7

Three months later, Derek stood at the window in his office and watched the sun set on another September day. September had not been a good month, and his frustration was evident in the clench of his jaw.

"I just don't understand," he complained to his brother without turning around.

"Exactly what has been happening?" Adam questioned. "A few weeks ago, you were so positive everything was going to work out just fine."

"That is the problem. Everything was perfect a few weeks ago. Nellie had left for a three-week vacation the night Tracey and I renewed our vows. That gave Tracey and I more time alone. It was great. We came to work together, even got in a few long lunches. We went home together, took that mangy beast for long walks on the beach, and cooked dinner together. Our evenings were full of cuddles and music. The woman even asked me for piano lessons, and we would play for hours together. Weekends, we played like kids. We've been to the zoo and SeaWorld. Although it's not to say we didn't have our squabbles, but they all ended peacefully. Nellie had been back about two weeks when everything began to fall apart." Even saying the problems aloud didn't make the understanding of the issues any easier. Derek ran a hand around the back of his neck as if to ease the knot of tension that had taken up residence there.

"You didn't by chance revert back to ordering her around, did you?" Adam had to ask because it appeared that Tracey's rebellious attitudes usually patterned around Derek's male chauvinistic streak.

"Not any more than usual." Derek gave his brother a slight grin. "That's where our squabbles usually start. No, this time it's different. One day, we were getting dressed to come into the office, and she came out of the shower stating she would rather drive herself in to work. I thought maybe she was meeting Christy or Susan for lunch or something, but from that day forward, she will neither drive to or go home from work with me."

"That doesn't sound like the ruination of your marriage. She probably just wants a little space from you. Like most of us from time to time."

"Adam, have I ever told you that your talents are wasted on the ranch and that you should go into show business?"

"Tsk, tsk tsk...so what else is up, brother of mine?"

"Well, if she gets home from work before I do, she's in the kitchen helping Nellie or in the den surrounded by papers. Each time, she's too busy to go with me to walk Barney. When I get back, nine times out of ten, she's had a late lunch and doesn't want dinner or just pushes her dinner around her plate. If I offer a piano lesson or invite her to listen to music or watch a movie, she says she's busy. No matter what I say, she says the opposite just to provoke an argument. When my temper gets the better of me and I explode, she tells me things aren't going to work out and that if we are going to separate in a few months anyway, then we should just go ahead and do it now. Then she asks if I wouldn't mind letting her move back into her old apartment.

I hate that apartment. She refused to let go of it when she moved in with me, stating she would need a place to go back to in a year. So to keep peace, I let her keep it. I even paid the blasted rent on it for the year. Now each time I refuse to let her move back into it, she gets worse. Darn it, Adam, she even starting to flinch or back away from me when I try and touch her."

"Maybe you did something to scare her sexually."

"I thought of that. I thought back, and she has always been an agreeable, active partner. I've never pushed or made her do anything she did not want or was not ready for. She still responds to my touch if I get her to hold still long enough to get my arms around her and kiss her, and currently, that's only when she is half asleep and just too fatigued to remember to fight me off."

"Have you just come right out and asked her what's up?"

"What do you think?" Derek's sarcasm slipped out. Then he shook it off. "Of course I asked her. She just tells me nothing is wrong. She just feels that if we are to go our separate ways in a few months, then we shouldn't get too used to each other."

"Well, if you want my opinion, little brother, she is either getting too used to you and is dangerously close to falling in love with you or she's hiding something, or both."

"Hiding what?"

"Something she figures you'll never find out about if she gets you mad enough to let her go."

"Well, that'll never happen. She can fight, kick, and scream all she wants, but I will never let her go. If she hiding something, I will find out what it is. She won't lie to me, you know, so all I have to do is ask the right questions. Do you any idea where I might start looking?"

The buzzer on Derek's intercom interrupted Adam as he was about to speak. Derek excused himself to answer it. "Yes?"

"Sorry to disturb you, Mr. Callahan, but Cindy, Mrs. Callahan's assistant, is asking to see you. She says it's important."

"Send her in."

"Anything wrong?" Adam questioned his brother as he hung up the phone.

"I'm not sure," he answered as Cindy walked in.

"Mr. Callahan, I'm so sorry to disturb you. Oh, I'm sorry, I didn't know you had company. I guess this can wait," she said as she backed toward the door.

"If you need to discuss company business with my brother, I can step out for a moment." Adam stood up.

"Well, it's not exactly company business. It's actually about Mrs. Callahan."

"Adam, you can stay. Cindy, you remember my brother Adam, and whether it's business or personal, I have don't have any secrets from him. So tell me, what's wrong?"

"Well, I'll probably be fired for breaking her confidence, but I am getting really worried about her."

"What is it about my wife that concerns you so much that you feel the need to break her confidence?"

"Well, you know she's had the flu lately, but she's been so sick. I mean this flu thing has lasted for a couple of weeks. She still can't keep anything down. She's been living on crackers and 7 Up, and even then, she doesn't always tolerate that well. I mean, you probably already know all this," she explained, so nervous about telling on her boss that she missed the looks passed between brothers. "But today…"

"What about today?" Derek prompted her, suddenly feeling anxious.

"Well, she's been sick all day. She can't keep anything down, and she's gotten so weak that I had to help her back to her desk the last time. When I asked her about coming to get you, she said she did not want to worry you and that with a little rest, she would be just fine. She said that she would even go home early today, as soon as we finish the Allen project. But sir, I don't think she should be driving in that condition."

"Thank you, Cindy. You did the right thing by coming and telling me. I'll go and talk to her," Derek told Cindy, placing a hand on her shoulder as he passed. "And don't worry, I'll let her think I was just stopping by her office to say hello. She'll never know you told me anything." With that, he left the office and strode quickly down the hall to his wife's office.

Adam followed more slowly, also stopping to reassure Cindy that all would be well and to thank her for her concern over his sister-in-law.

By this time, Tracey had lain her head down on the arm that rested on her desk, closing her eyes in the hopes that the room would stop spinning. When she heard the door opening, she didn't even bother picking her head up since she was only expecting Cindy; everyone else knocked. "Don't panic, Cindy. I'm just resting for a few minutes. Give me five, then come back, and we'll finish that report. Okay?"

"How about I give you five seconds, just five seconds to tell me just what the heck is going on?" Derek demanded.

Tracey jerked her head up at the sound of his voice. When she did, the room began to spin again at her sudden movement. She grabbed for the desk to steady her world and tried to smile. "Hello, Derek."

"Don't hello me. Start talking, woman."

"Calm down. I just have a little headache." It wasn't a complete lie. She did have a headache; it was at least a partial truth.

"A little headache, my foot. You're so pale your skin is almost translucent. You have circles under your eyes that are so bruised that you look as if you've been on the losing end of a street fight. A good wind, my love, would blow you away. You need to go see a doctor."

"I will. I even have an appointment after work. So now will you go away? I have work to do."

"Sorry, but you are done for the day. You are going in immediately for a checkup. Get your things."

"I have my own car. I will go when I am ready."

"You are ready now, and you have two options. One is to get up right now and come with me on your own, or two, I can pick you up and carry you."

Adam, sensing a major argument about to erupt, stepped into the room. "Tracey, he's not issuing an idle threat."

"Reinforcements?" Tracey asked sarcastically, looking from one brother to the other.

"When dealing with you, I need all the help I can get. Now let's go."

"I hate you."

"So you've told me before, and I would stand here and argue the point, but I'd rather get you to a doctor. I am, however, going to give you to the count of three to make a decision on your own. Otherwise, I'll make it for you," Derek told her, already coming around her desk and sliding the rolling chair away from the desk, turning it in preparation for making good on his threat.

"Oh, all right, I'll go home. But," she began as she bent over to get her purse from the drawer, "I won't go with you. Adam, will you drive me home please?"

Adam never had a chance to respond because as Tracey stood upright, she lost her battle with the dizziness and quietly passed out, right into her husband's arms.

Derek caught her to him and scooped her up into his arms. "Stubborn witch."

As Derek carried her out the door, he saw that Cindy was back at her desk. "Cindy, do you know the name of her doctor?"

"Yes, sir."

"Please call him and ask him to meet us at the emergency room at Scripts hospital," he ordered and did not wait for a response. Adam stopped to thank her before hurrying after his brother.

Tracey's eyes fluttered open as Derek lowered her gently into the car. "What happened?"

"You passed out, honey. Just lay back and rest," he ordered her in a semistern voice, but tempered even that with a soft kiss.

Too weak to object, she obeyed. Closing her eyes, she decided that between the office and home, she would be able to think of some way to get him to return to the office so she could take care of herself.

Unfortunately, when the car stopped, she was still too weak to offer more than a murmured objection as he lifted her from the car. "Go ahead and grumble. When you are strong enough to stand on her your own two feet, I might be persuaded to actually listen," he told her, but she had fainted once again, her head resting on his chest.

The nurse saw them coming and motioned for them to follow her into a room. Once in the room, he gently laid her on the bed. "Her doctor has been called and should be on his way." With a nod, the nurse took down all the information that Derek could tell her and then made quick work of taking Tracey's vital signs. "Now why don't you go back out to the desk and get all the paperwork completed? I will look after your wife."

Reluctantly, he left and did as he was asked. Adam joined his brother at the admitting counter, worry etched on his face. "How is she?"

"Out cold again. She comes around for a few moments, then she passes out again. I don't know what's wrong, so I don't know if she's all right."

"She's a tough lady. I'm sure she'll be just fine. Like Cindy said, it's probably the flu, or maybe your chauvinistic ways gave her an ulcer. Either one is quickly cured." He tried to make Derek smile, but the man's mind was still back in the room with his wife.

Derek turned to look at his brother, tears of worry actually filling his eyes. "She has to get better. I don't know what I would do without her in my life. Every day, I fall more in love with her."

"Have you told her that?"

"I would have if I thought it would help, but I'm afraid it'll just add more pressure on her." Terror clenched his heart as he signed the papers giving the hospital emergency room permission to treat his wife.

The doctor came by and stopped long enough to introduce himself and ask some questions about her symptoms.

"We'll have your wife feeling better in just a little while, and if I know Tracey, she'll be chomping at the bit in a couple of hours to get out of here. However, since she has lost consciousness, I will probably want to keep her in for observation for the night at least. But we'll see." With that, the doctor left them to tend to Tracey, leaving behind two very puzzled men.

"Sounds like he already knows what's wrong with her," Derek commented in confusion.

"He probably does." Adam grinned at his obtuse brother.

"Maybe she has a history of ulcers or something, and I have aggravated it. Maybe I *have* been too rough on her," Derek rambled on, ignoring Adam, who, with an indulgent smile, just sat back and listened. Finally, Derek, unable to wait any longer, got up and headed back to his wife, wanting—no, needing to be with her. However, once at the doorway, the conversation inside the room brought him up short.

"You know, Tracey, I told you if the nausea got any worse, you were to come back in and see me. There are medications that help with this."

"I know, but I don't want to take medications. I don't want the baby harmed."

"The baby will be fine. I would never give you anything that would harm your child. However, you need to remember that the baby takes its nourishment from you and will always take what it needs, but if you are unable to replenish your reserves, you are the one who will suffer. However, when you suffer too much, then so does that child."

"I—" Tracey began. Derek moved aside the curtain that had kept him from their view.

"A baby? You're pregnant? Is that why you have been so sick?" he demanded.

"Thanks a lot, doc," Tracey muttered as she grimaced against the anger in Derek's voice.

"Good Lord, Tracey, don't tell me that you haven't told your husband you're pregnant? How did you get away with that, since you have not had such an easy time of it?"

"Oh, doctor, she's very clever," Derek answered for her, anger turning his soft gray eyes to cold steel as they looked at her. "Almost too clever, but now that her secret is out, she'll be watched much, much closer." His words left no doubt in Tracey's mind that they were not just a threat but also a promise. Escape would no longer be an option.

"Glad to hear it. She needs to take much better care of herself if this baby is to be born healthy, as well as having a mother around to take care of it. I am going to go ahead and admit her for the night and pump her full of fluids. That should stabilize her. If her lab work is okay in the morning and she can tolerate at least a bland diet, then she can go home, but I will want to see her once a week until I am sure she's passed through this phase."

"But I have a meeting tomorrow," Tracey complained.

"You will follow doctor's orders." Derek's tone of voice left no room for objections.

The doctor was nodding in agreement as he added, "Tracey, you need rest. I am recommending a minimum of two weeks off work. See me then about returning."

"No way," she told both men adamantly.

"I'll take care of this," Derek informed the doctor. Turning to his wife, he continued, "Consider yourself on immediate medical separation from the company. Your rehire will be reevaluated by the board of directors when and *if* I ever feel you are fit enough to return to work."

"You can't do that! You keep telling me I own half of it."

"You own half of Callahan Architectures. Adam, Jon, and I own Callahan Incorporated. Therefore, I can do anything I want, and I want you to follow doctor's orders."

The doctor cleared his throat, trying desperately to hide his smile. "Well, as things appear to be under control here, I'll go arrange your admission and leave you two alone for a while."

"No!" Tracey turned to the doctor frantically; being alone with the man who looked this dangerous would not be good, at least for her." Please, please if you're going to make me stay, tell them I can't have any visitors, especially him." She pointed at Derek.

"Tracey, I think you have had enough time alone. I think he might be a much better medicine for you than any I can prescribe."

"Thank you, doctor. I appreciate your coming in so quickly. When you arrange for that room, can you make it a private one? I plan on staying here with her for the night," Derek spoke to the doctor, ignoring Tracey's obvious panic.

"I'll see what I can do. And, Tracey, I'll see you later this evening to see how you're coming along."

After the doctor left them alone, Derek went around to the side of the bed that did not have the intravenous tubing hanging in his way. Trying to assemble his thoughts, Derek studied the fluids that were dripping into the tube that was already helping Tracey come back to life, back to him.

"I don't know whether to beat you or hug you."

"How about going away and leaving me alone?"

"Not an option," he told her as he sat down on the bed beside her. "You honestly weren't going to tell me about the baby, were you?"

The hurt in his voice was almost her undoing. She bit down on her lip to keep from talking and rolled away from him. It was hard enough to hear the hurt. She just couldn't face it head-on, at least not right now, and she was too tired to be strong.

"You're going to have to talk to me sooner or later."

The nurse came in then and ordered him to go to the admissions office again and get the additional paperwork completed while she got Tracey ready to be transported to her room.

Derek bent over Tracey and brushed away the loose strands of hair that lay against her pale cheek. Kissing her lightly, he said, "I'll be right back. And we will talk about it then." Then he left the room.

Once Tracey was in her room, the nurses put her through the admitting rituals. She was exhausted. However, sleep was not an option because she knew she needed to gather her strength. Derek would be there soon, and she was going to have to try and explain herself, and although she knew he deserved answers, she had no idea what to say to him.

After a while, her eyes began to close slowly. Heavy with fatigue and against her will, she fell asleep. It was dark when she awoke, but her eyes immediately found Derek; he stood by the window. His hurt and confusion were almost palpable. Her eyes burned with tears, knowing she had caused his pain and that she had done it deliberately.

As if sensing her stare, he turned toward her slowly. "Feeling better?" he asked gently.

"Yes, thank you."

"Why do I have a feeling that if you were feeling worse, you would never tell me?"

"I'd never lie to you."

"No, but you would hold information from me and do everything in your power to keep me in the dark."

Tracey bit down on her lip to keep from crying; she had brought this on and would now have to live with the consequences.

"Damn it, Tracey!" he began, and she knew he must be angry because he never cursed. "I deserved to know you were pregnant with my child."

Tracey had one shot left at making him angry enough to walk away from her, at least long enough for her to go far enough away where she could protect her heart. "What makes you think it's your baby?"

Instead of getting angry, he just smiled at her. "So you've been sleeping with other men since we've been married?"

"Of course not."

"Then it's mine."

"I could have gotten pregnant before we ever went to Las Vegas, you know."

"Ordinarily, that might be true, but you didn't because you went to Vegas a virgin."

"You can't prove that."

"Honey, that only goes to prove just how innocent you were. So you want proof, huh?" Derek sat down beside her and reached an arm across her, placing it down on the blanket, effectively pinning her in place. "One, you have always been an active member of the church, and I know your beliefs. We do go to the same church, remember? Two, most of your social life consisted of parties and social events with our best friends or the church. I never saw you once with a date. Three, the blood spots on the sheets in our hotel room in Vegas were a dead giveaway. There is also the fact that you were and still are amazed at the response I can elicit from you when we make love. If you had been use to having *sex*, some things would not have come as a surprise. Now I can probably go on. Do you need me to?"

Tracey shook her head as her cheeks burned with embarrassment. Thinking quickly, she tried again, "I could have—"

"Could have what? Been on your cycle while in Vegas? Then you still could not have been pregnant before Vegas, before we got married, because by your own admission, you have not been with anyone since. The child is mine. Going to concede now, or do I have to go on?"

"I hate you."

"Now where have I heard that before? Give up?" He knew the baby was his. He had no doubt in his mind, but for some reason, he felt the need to push her into saying so.

"It's my baby."

"I realize that, honey, but you did not get in this condition alone, unless you have been perfecting the art of osmosis?"

"Please, Derek, leave me alone. I'm tired," she told him, wanting to turn away from him but could not because he had her trapped within the blanket, so when unwanted tears burned her eyes, she just closed them.

"Haven't you learned yet? I am not going to leave you alone. No matter how mad you make me, I am not going to let you out of our agreement."

Her tears finally pushed past her closed eyes, and when Derek lifted his hand to brush them away, the hold he had on her also lifted, and she turned away from him.

"Someday, you are also going to learn you can't run away from me in body or in mind, because I won't let you. You are carrying my child, and I love you both too much to ever let you go." There, he had said it. He had finally told her he loved her. He should have felt happy or relieved—something other than the hurt he felt as Tracey just began to cry all the harder.

"Tracey, honey, what's the matter? Please talk to me," Derek pleaded with her, but when her crying began to border on hysteria, Derek reached for the nurses call bell and summoned help.

After the nurse had given Tracey a mild sedative, Tracey's crying slowly subsided, and she fell into a fitful sleep.

This time, when she woke, she found Jon, Derek's younger brother, lounging in the chair beside her bed.

"Hello, Sleeping Beauty."

"Hello, Jon." She smiled gently at her brother-in-law. "What are you doing here?"

"Derek didn't want you to be alone, and Adam had to get back to the baby, so he called me. He thought you might not want to see him right now. You know, I'm a good listener. Care to tell me about what caused that major crying episode?"

"I have no idea why I behaved so irrationally. I think I was just too tired to deal with your brother at the time. I mean, I've been wrong before, and although I don't like admitting to it, I always do, but…" She blushed and chewed nervously on her lip.

"But usually, they are honest mistakes, and this time?"

"This time, I have no excuse—or at least an excuse that makes any sense. I hurt him."

"Yes, you did," he answered her bluntly, making her wince. Then he softened the blow by adding, "But he'll survive, or rather, he will if you are willing to give in a little on this."

"I have made such a mess of things," she told him in a voice just above a whisper. "You know, he told me he loves me."

"He does."

"No, he doesn't. He may think he does because I am carrying his child and thinks he has to. I do believe he loves this child already, simply because it is a part of him. I was wrong in trying to hide it from him. But he does not love me for me." She waved Jon back when he would have objected. "It's okay, Jon. I'm okay with it now. I promise I will not try and keep him or any of you away from this child." She lay back against the pillows with a sigh. "I just wish—" she began and then stopped.

"Tracey, I can't explain it right now, but I understand what you two are going through. You can talk to me, you know. Maybe I can help. Tell me, what do you wish?"

"I just wish—" She shook her head and smiled. "Never mind. Isn't wishing for the unattainable how they came up with the expression 'If wishes were horses, all beggars would ride?' So for me, it needs to be my two feet on the ground. No wishing, no regrets. Did Derek go home?"

"Are you kidding? He is currently wearing a hole in the carpet of the waiting room at the end of the hall. Would you like me to go and get him?"

"Honestly?" She gave her brother-in-law a sad smile. "No. I'd like to know he went home and was getting some rest. He looked so tired earlier. Then he could come back when both of us are rested enough to deal with the issues. But realistically, I know neither of us is going to rest until all this is settled, so if I don't deal with this now, all we'll be more tired and irritable."

"Smart woman," Jon told her. He got up from the chair to drop a kiss on her cheek. "No wonder my brother married you."

"He married me on accident, and now he'll stay married because of another one."

Jon just shook his head—two steps forward and one step back. "You two are going to be the death of all of us who love you," he teased her before patting her tummy. "Good night, little nephew. Just ignore your parents right now. They've both lost their minds."

Tracey just slapped his hand away. "Hey, it's never too early to talk to a baby." He grinned at her. "Okay, Beauty, I'm going for the beast. Any last words?"

"Care to help me make a run for it?"

"And face the wrath of Derek the barbarian? Not me, I'm a coward," he said as he was leaving, trying to make her laugh. He was finally rewarded with a small smile.

Slowly, her smile faded. Swallowing her pride and admitting she was wrong had never been easy for her, but this time, her pride had hurt the man she loved more than life itself. She knew she deserved all of his anger. However, knowing she deserved something didn't make her any less nervous about receiving it.

A few minutes later, Derek came into the room and found the bed empty. A quick look around found Tracey making her way very slowly back toward it.

"Are you supposed to be out of bed?"

"Probably not," she replied honestly. Her knees began to shake with weakness. "Oh no," she began as she looked up at him. "Derek?"

"Yes?"

"Help," she said as her knees turned to water.

A few steps, and Derek caught her and easily lifted her up into his arms. He carried her over to the bed and reluctantly laid her down. After covering her up with the blanket, he started to step back and was surprised to find her hand on his arm.

"Thank you." Simple words, but the smile that accompanied them was enough to melt the last of his hurt and anger.

"Is it okay if I sit with you?" he asked, and at her nod, he went to move to the chair Jon had just vacated, but she moved over and patted the bed beside her.

As he sat down, he took her hand in his. "Tracey…"

"Derek…"

They had both spoken together and then stopped, giving the other a chance to speak first. The silence stretched on until finally Derek gave in. "Tracey, I am so sorry for getting you so upset. It's just that I—"

Tracey reached up and placed a finger against his lips, interrupting him. "No. This time, you have nothing to apologize for. I do." She bit down on her lip to keep it from quivering. Sitting up, she pulled her hand from his and placed both her hands on his cheeks. "My actions hurt and scared you. I have probably done stupider things in my life, although I am not sure when, but this time, I really screwed up, and I am sorry. I promise I will honor our agreement until the end of the year. Please do not feel you have to tell me you love me just because you think I have to hear the words."

"But, Tracey," he tried to interrupt her, but she just shook her head.

"It's okay, honestly. Knowing that you will love our baby and will make a wonderful father to her is enough. We made a good start on being friends, and I would like us to keep going in that vein. Then when we do go our separate ways, our child will have the best of both of us." Tears fell unchecked down her cheeks as her heart broke in two. "Please tell me you forgive me for being such a shrew."

"Oh, honey, you are not a shrew." He smiled down at her. "A hot-tempered, stubborn Irish woman, but never a shrew." He teased a small smile from her. "Are you ready to tell me why you felt the need to hide the pregnancy from me?"

Tracey's smile faded, and a new wave of tears fell. "I can't," she whispered, and he didn't push. Instead he gathered her closer in his arms. "It's okay. Maybe someday, you'll trust me enough to tell me. For now, I'll settle for holding you."

She snuggled closer to him and felt his lips dropping kisses on the top of her head. "I've missed you. I've missed this," he told her quietly.

She nodded in understanding. She had missed this warm gentleness. Then she thought that if she missed him and his touches that bad when she was still living with him, how was she going to survive when their year was up? Before the thought could depress her further, Derek tipped her head up and claimed her lips in a deep soul-searching, soul-refreshing kiss.

This was how Jon found them a few minutes later when he opened the door to the room to make sure all was well. With a grin, he backed out of the door. Neither one of the occupants had even noticed him. With a quick thumbs-up toward the heavens, he whispered, "And another battle ends in victory. Thanks for your help."

Sid and Charlie both gave a sigh of relief. "If I wasn't already a spirit, I think those two would have given me a heart attack by now."

"Yeah, it was pretty smart move on your part, though, knocking the wind literally out from under her. At least we have them talking again."

"Yeah, but talking is not communicating. We are going to have to get awfully creative before these two boneheads finally figure out what has been under their noses for all these years."

"Job security, Charlie. Job security."

8

A few weeks later, Tracey was sitting in the kitchen talking to Nellie and trying to help with dinner preparations. "Are you sure I can't do something to help?"

"I'm sure. You just sit there and keep me company while you eat your afternoon snack. Then go and get yourself a little nap."

"Man, oh man. You would think I was the baby—not carrying one—with all the naps I've been taking."

"Well, considering you are supposed to be taking a morning and an afternoon nap both, and you haven't done that yet"—Nellie paused to give her a stern, motherly look—"I wouldn't complain too loudly."

Derek chose that moment to walk into the kitchen, and Tracey's head snapped up guiltily her fork halfway to her mouth.

"Yes, Tracey, complain too loudly, and your husband, coming home early, may accidentally over hear you and know that you have been disobeying doctor's orders, again." He stood there looking at her with his arms crossed against his chest.

"Oh, look, Nellie. Derek's home early. Hi, what are you doing home?" Evasion was a good plan; it was short-lived, but it was a good plan nonetheless.

"I came home to spend some time with my wife, the same wife who was complaining about being bored because all she was allowed to do was sleep and eat."

"Well, that's true."

He raised a questioning eyebrow at her. "If you're not sleeping in the morning and waiting until"—he glanced up at the clock—"three thirty in the afternoon to take a nap, probably a short one, what are you doing with your time?" He held up a hand, stopping her from answering right away. "And before you say, 'Nothing,' I might point out the streaks of dirt on your clothes and the cute one across your cheek."

She put her fork down and rubbed a guilty hand across her cheek, looking over at Nellie, who had turned away. "Traitor," she whispered before turning her most dazzling fake smile on her husband. The baby was his soft spot; use it to your best advantage, she told herself. "I was just sorting through the spare room—you know, the one you wanted to turn into a nursery?" See? How could he get mad? She was doing something for his child, easy.

At her words, Derek began ranting and raving, and Tracey dropped her head into her hand in defeat. How could she do something so strenuous, especially when the doctor wanted her resting? If she wanted the room cleared out, all she had to do was tell him, and he would have done it for her, or he could have hired a crew to do it. He just couldn't believe she wouldn't behave for once. When he finally wound down, she looked up at him. "Done?"

"For the moment."

"Okay."

"Okay what?" he asked her suspiciously

"Okay, you win. I promise I won't clean the room any-more," she said. It was an easy promise to keep because the room was done.

Derek looked at his wife first and then over at Nellie, whose shoulders were looking suspiciously like they were shaking with laughter. "For some reason, I don't think I 'won' anything at all, but that you still have the upper hand here. However, on the premise that I won, at least for now, I'll settle for a kiss as my prize." He shook his head in abject resignation at the two women before cap-turing Tracey's lips for a kiss.

"Mmm, you taste like apples and cinnamon." He kissed her again.

"I should." She laughed and used her fork to point at her plate.

"Apple pie? Is that on your diet?"

"My diet says, 'An afternoon snack of fruit.' This *is* fruit."

"It's pie. Where is the protein drink you are supposed to be having with your snacks? The one I make up for you each morning?"

Tracey nibbled on her lips before answering, "Uh, in the refrigerator?"

"You need to be drinking it."

"Derek, that stuff is gross. I don't know what you put in it, and frankly, I really don't want to know."

"You need the nutritional value in it."

"Come on, I've finally stopped throwing everything up, and that stuff will just start the process all over again."

"It is good for you and the baby," he told her. He went to retrieve the drink from the refrigerator, placed it back on the blender base, and power blasted it a couple of times to remix it for her. Pouring some into a glass, he placed the glass and a banana in front of her, taking away her plate of apple pie. "There, eat that. Much better for you both," he told her, then promptly finished off her plate.

"Hey, how come you get to eat that?"

"Because I am not pregnant, and I am already healthy and strong. You are not."

"I don't think I like you very much."

"That's okay. I like you enough for both of us," he teased her as he kissed her pouting lips. "I'll tell you what, you sit here and finish up your snack, and I'll play lady's maid and draw you a nice warm bath."

"Are you trying to tell me I'm dirty?"

"Honey, I would never say anything that crude," he told her as he walked to the kitchen door, and just as he was about to close the door, he added, "I'd say you were filthy." He ducked out just as the napkin holder off the table slammed into the wood.

"Nellie, this stuff even smells awful. How am I supposed to drink it without gagging?" Tracey complained after Derek had left.

Nellie reached over and took the glass and replaced it with a glass of milk and then traded the banana for another slice of pie. "The same way you have been drinking it for the last two weeks." Nellie gave her a wink before pouring it down the sink.

"Oh, Nellie, I love you."

"Go on with you now. Just finish up before he comes back and finds out. Then we'll both be out in the doghouse with Barney."

Tracey made quick work of the snack and gave Nellie a quick hug before leaving the kitchen.

When she got upstairs, she found the bedroom deserted and wandered into the bathroom. There, the huge garden tub was filled with bubbles and…"Derek?"

"Well, you were complaining about being treated like a baby, and since I was drawing my baby a bath, I figured you needed a toy, and when I couldn't find a rubber ducky, I improvised."

She laughed. "You are a little bigger than a rubber ducky," she said as she sat on the edge of the bathtub.

"True. But I'm a lot more fun than a rubber ducky." With that, he grabbed her and dragged her into the tub, clothes and all.

"Derek!" she squealed, but his mouth cut off any more objections. Tracey had no idea that a bath could be so much fun or so sensual. By the time Derek let her climb from the tub, she doubted she would ever look at a bubble bath in quite the same way again.

However, once out of the bath, Tracey had asked for a little privacy to dress, so with one last kiss, Derek sat out on the balcony to wait for her, a smile of happy contentment on his face. Life was good. He was going to be a father in a few months, and the woman of his heart actually seemed too happy to be in his home. She hadn't mentioned leaving him once since the night she had spent in the hospital. Yes, life was good.

Thump!

"Hey!" Derek yelled as Tracey pulled back the pillow to hit him again. Catching the pillow midair, he pulled it and her into his arms. "What did you do that for?"

"You made me fat!"

"What? What are you talking about?" he asked as he finally pulled the pillow from her grip and threw it back into the room.

"You and your stupid diet! I've gained too much weight, and now I can't get into my favorite jeans."

"Is that all?" Someday, Derek would learn what *not* to say to a pregnant woman—if he lived that long.

Tracey began stomping around dressed only in her underclothes and one of his sweatshirts. She ranted and raved about bossy men who used high-handed ways to make stupid requests like making her eat three meals and three snacks a day. It was a wonder that they didn't have to roll her around the house.

Tracey continued to rant as she stormed back into the house and began throwing clothes out of her drawer at Derek, clothes she insisted were now a waste of money because she would never fit into them again.

Derek easily caught the clothes and methodically refolded them, letting her go on until she seemed to run out of steam. "Done?" he asked, a smile twitching on his lips.

"Don't you dare laugh at me! Since I have been just hanging lazily around the house, all I've worn is sweats and T-shirts. I had no idea I'd gained so much weight. Why didn't you tell me I was getting fat?"

"You are not fat, silly, you're pregnant, and there is a difference, you know. Besides, I didn't tell you anything because, well, I like seeing you plump up a bit." Open mouth, insert foot.

"Plump? I'm plump?"

"No, no, honey. I didn't mean it that way. I mean you had lost so much weight when you were sick it has been nice to see you fill out and even begin to get a tummy because…" Tracey's face told him he was not getting out of the hole but digging himself in deeper. *Okay, Lord, how do I get out of this one?* he asked silently and desperately.

∽

"So, Charlie, think we should help him out?"

"No."

"Well, he should think before he speaks. But he really means well."

"True. Oh, all right, this time."

∽

"Derek, it's way too soon for me to be showing. So from now on, when it comes to food, I am not going to listen to you."

"You know, my little love, you may think it's too early to show, but if you actually look at yourself, you are not fat. In fact, you are still almost too slender, and the scale shows you are not even up to the weight you were when we got married. That's a baby tummy. Are you saying you are unhappy with being pregnant?"

"Of course not." She actually loved the idea of being pregnant with Derek's child. She just was vain enough to want to stay slender and pretty for him too. "It's just that…" *I'm afraid you won't fall in love with me if I don't look good to you*, she told herself.

Her hesitation gave him the time to get close to her, tipping her chin up so she could see his sincerity as he spoke. "You are beautiful, and everyday that my child grows inside you, the more beautiful you are. I am looking forward to the day when I can place my hand on your tummy and feel my son come to life." Then he knelt down in front of her, lifting the sweatshirt up he ran his hand over the slight swelling of her stomach. "Okay, my son, it's up to you and me to convince your mommy that she is absolutely gorgeous and always will be to the men in her life." He began raining butterfly kisses on her stomach until she pushed him away, laughing.

"Stop that! I'm mad at you," she told him, trying to insert a still-mad tone in her voice and failing miserably.

"Still? I guess I'll just have to..." He pressed the area behind her knees, making her legs fold and landing her right in his lap.

"Hey, that's not fair. You are using brute force on my *daughter* and me." She pushed at his shoulders.

"No, it's just that my *son* and I outnumber you." He held her fast in his arms.

"Daughter."

"Son." He kissed the tip of her nose.

"Daughter." She nipped at his nose.

"Son." He nuzzled her neck.

"Daughter," she breathed out huskily.

"Fine," he pretended to give in as he captured her lips before adding, "you can have one of each."

"Bite your tongue," she replied, then suited actions to words, nipping his tongue gently with hers.

"So you don't want to talk anymore, huh? Okay, have it your way," he told her as he suited actions to words and stopped talking; he just showed her how he felt. Dinner could wait.

Tracey had been afraid her increasing size would make Derek turn away from her, no matter what he had said that first night when she could no longer fit in her jeans. However, over the next few months, as her stomach continued to grow like a slowly inflating beach ball, so did his warm gentleness. He made love to her with such tender reverence that he made her feel beautiful and cherished. Thus, she fell deeper and deeper in love with the man of her dreams, her heart.

"Close call."

"It wasn't quite his time to join us." Charlie grinned. "Yet."

9

Christmas is a wonderful magical time, a time for family and friends, a time for giving. *Unless you were a couple of stubborn, pigheaded people who still continue to fail at communication 101,* Nellie thought as she watched Tracey and Derek at it again.

"The doctor gave me permission to fly. I'm only six months along. I'm going home for Christmas."

"It's not the flying that I am talking about, and you know it. It's been a tradition for as long as I can remember that no matter how far away the family may be during the year, every Christmas, we gather at the ranch and have an old-fashioned Christmas. I want to continue that tradition with my wife."

"I am not stopping you from your traditions. In fact, I don't want you to miss Christmas with your family. You go home to your family, and I will go home to mine. We'll meet back here afterwards."

"That is not how a husband and wife spend Christmas."

"It is for this kind of husband and wife. We have never spent a Christmas together before. And we will never again, so why bother with this year?"

"This could be the first of many if you would be reasonable."

"I am being reasonable, and if you would stop being so thickheaded, you would see it too."

"All I see is a woman who is still running away."

"I am not running away. I said I was coming back. Now if you will excuse me, I have to get my reservation in. There is only three weeks left until Christmas, and seats are going to be hard to get. After that, I have an appointment with Christine to find some kind of formal dress for the company Christmas party, one that will fit over this belly." She patted her round tummy, drawing Derek's attention from the argument.

His anger faded as he looked at his child growing inside the woman he loved. Should he give in? She had not fought him so hard over anything in months. He could let her call for the reservations and pray there was no seat available. He could do anything but let her go.

"Why don't we just fly your family down here? There's plenty of room at the ranch."

"No."

Why?"

"Because my family has their own traditions and… and… oh, just because."

"Fine. Call. Make the reservations, just make them for two. I'll go with you instead."

"No. I am serious about this. I am going to spend Christmas with my family, and you will go spend Christmas with yours, period," she told him with a firm determined voice, far from what she was actually feeling.

"This is not over yet, Tracey," he called after her as she walked away and went into the den.

"Want to bet?" she told him as she closed the door with a resounding click.

"Yes, I do," he said aloud. "And you, my little witch, will lose," he added to the closed door. Turning, he saw Nellie in the kitchen door and gave her a helpless shrug.

"Mighty interesting mating dance you two perform," she told him with a shake of her head, and as she turned back toward the kitchen, she added, "daily."

"I get enough lip from one lady in this house. I don't need two of you."

"Sure you do. You would be lost without either one of us."

"Lord, help me," Derek looked up and pleaded.

"He did. He sent you Tracey."

"Yeah," Derek conceded. Then with a rueful smile as he looked at the closed den door, he added, "But he forgot to send the instruction manual."

"It's there. You just need to learn how to read it," Nellie told him and then left the room.

Derek looked from the now-closed kitchen door to the still-closed den door and growled. "Well, fine then. Leave me out here alone. I think better in the quiet anyway."

Frustrated, he went back to his chair and picked up the newspaper he had been reading before the battle had begun; first, he prayed for Tracey's failure at finding airline seats. Then he started looking through the paper as if it would give him some answers.

Tracey hadn't failed; in fact, she had gotten everything she had wanted that morning, but when she went out to meet Christine for lunch with what should have been a feeling of triumph, she realized what she was actually feeling was the opposite.

"What's the matter, Tracey? You're looking a little down."

"Oh, nothing that a little shopping won't fix. First, we'll get the dress issue out of the way. Then we can hit the stores for a little Christmas splurging."

"Now, Tracey, about this dress. Please tell me you are not planning on doing what you did before? I thought Jon was going to kill me for aiding and abetting you."

"No, I am serious this time. Besides, if you want my interpretation of Jon's reaction, he did not want to kill you. He wanted something a whole lot different."

Christine blushed furiously. "I don't know what you are talking about. He just likes to boss me around. He's the youngest Callahan brother and needed someone to be a big bossy brother to, so when I moved in to the ranch next door, I became his target. Although sometimes, I wish—" Christine broke off with a sigh.

"What do you wish for, Christine?"

"I wish you were right and that he wanted something more than wanting to take care of me, to big brother me to death."

"Have you ever told him how you feel?"

"I'll answer that if you answer that about you and Derek."

"I think it's time to go shopping," Tracey said and pushed back her chair.

"That's what I thought. Come on, my friend, I found the most gorgeous dress the other day and ordered it in your size. Let's go see if we're on the same wavelength there too."

It was by a mutually unspoken agreement they both agreed to drop the subject of their unrequited love for the Callahan men.

By the time Tracey arrived home laden with packages, she was grateful to see that Derek seemed to have gotten over his earlier anger.

"After dinner, I thought we would go out and look for a tree," Derek brought up casually.

"Do you really want to go to all that trouble since neither of us will be home for Christmas?"

"It's only a decoration, Tracey. You've gone home for Christmas every year. Did you have a tree in your apartment?"

"Well, yes."

"And I have always gone home, but I have also always had one here. Besides, the Christmas season just doesn't feel like Christmas without one," he told her. Then he gave her a casual shrug as he added, "But if you really don't want one, we don't have to." His tone was tinged with the sound of a sad, disappointed little boy.

"No, we can go get a tree. It's not a big deal. Besides, tree lots always smell so wonderful." She gave in, but she had a feeling she had been cleverly manipulated.

It was the same feeling she would get off and on for the next two weeks. When they went shopping for the tree, they not only bought a tree, they also bought enough greenery to fill the whole house with the holiday pine smell. A few days later, they went shopping for his family and hers, deliberately spoiling the children. So much spoiling that after they wrapped the gifts, Derek said he would go ahead and ship her presents to her family because there were too many for her to carry on the plane.

Derek hung lights under Tracey's guidance and sat with her on the couch as he bragged about his handiwork. On most of the evenings before Christmas, he played the piano for her and coerced her into singing Christmas carols with him, entertaining themselves and Nellie.

Then the sun finally set on the evening of the company Christmas party. The moon rose in a night sky that was clear and bright with twinkling stars, but as far as Derek was concerned as he watched his wife come down the stairs toward him, the sky paled in comparison to her.

The dress that Christine had found had been perfect. Like the sky outside, the dress was midnight-blue velvet that matched the blue in her eyes. The empire waist had diamond like stones that drew the observers' eyes to her slenderness and not the rounding tummy below. Stepping up, he reached out to take her hand, pulling her to him.

He placed his hand on the nape of her neck, cradling her head in his hands. Tracey had pulled the front of her hair back with a rhinestone clip, leaving the rest of her hair cascading in long curls down her back to her waist. Derek knew that she had done that for him, and he felt his heart swell with love and hope.

Bending his head, he lightly kissed her temple. "You are so beautiful. I will be the envy of all the men at the party." His warm breath fanned her hair as he spoke.

Tracey shook her head and looked up at him. She too had been impressed as she had come downstairs to find Derek looking so handsome in his white dinner jacket. "No, I think I will be the envy of the woman at the party."

"You know, this could pose a problem."

"Oh really? How?"

"Well, causing all that jealousy. It would never do to have discontent in the office, so I was thinking, maybe we should just stay here and have our own little party."

"And not have the boss show up? No, I don't think so. This is the one time of year they feel on equal footing with you, and I would never want to be responsible for disappointing them. Besides, you paid a fortune for this dress. I should at least show it off once."

"So Christine blabbed huh?"

"Oh, yes, she was supposed to run my credit card, then wait for me to leave, then put through a credit, and then run yours."

"She always was such a snitch," Derek commented. "Mad?"

"I should be, but I felt I owed you one."

"Only one?"

"Yes. Now we are even."

"We'll see. But back to the subject at hand, I have no problem with paying three times the amount, even if it was just for me, because I could hold you like this forever."

"Forever?"

"Yes, Tracey, forever. What will it take to convince you that I—"

Tracey placed her fingers against his lips. "No, Derek, please don't spoil the evening by saying things that you feel you have to say." When he would have protested, she shook her head. "Please."

Derek kissed the fingers against his lips before pulling her hand away. He gave her a gallant bow before kissing the back of her hand in a courtly gesture. "Okay, Cinderella, tonight, we play it your way."

"Then, to the ball Prince Charming, to the ball." And to the ball they went, to laugh and dance and play the part of the perfect couple. The couples around them did envy them, not for the wonderful clothes or their good looks, but for the aura of love that surrounded them. Unfortunately, they were the only ones who could not see that beautiful aura.

A few days after the party, Tracey began packing for her trip home, part of her glad to be going. She needed to put some distance between her heart and Derek. Every day, she found her heart getting a little more out of control, so being away from him for a few days would give her time to tighten her resolve. However, she was feeling almost hurt that Derek had given in so easy about her leaving. For a man who had such *strong* opposition at one time, he was nearly bending over backward to send her on her way. Was he finally realizing that he wanted to be free? That she had been right and that he did not really love her but only the baby?

"Ready?" Derek asked from the doorway. He smiled as he watched her quickly brush the tears from her eyes.

"Yes, all I have to do is lock this last bag." She suited actions to words.

"Good, we wouldn't want you to miss your flight. Now you are sure your father is going to get out of court in time to pick you up from the airport?"

"He said it would be no problem. Although I am sure that if he got tied up, he would send Ann."

"Great. Let's go."

Derek picked up her bags and went down the stairs, leaving her to follow. "Well, fine, if you are so anxious to get rid of me, then maybe I just won't come back," she muttered unhappily. Once downstairs, tears burned her eyes again as she hugged Nellie good-bye.

Derek was bright and talkative as he drove her to the airport, seemingly oblivious to her questioning stares and silence. He kept up the chatter through the long wait to check in her baggage.

"I need your name, flight information, and number of bags to check," the attendant said as they stepped up to the counter.

"Tracey Callahan, flight 1812, United Airlines to San Francisco, and two bags," Tracey told her as she handed over her tickets. The attendant ran her information into the system

"I'm sorry, Mrs. Callahan, but it appears that your reservations have been canceled."

"Excuse me? I have tickets for this flight. They are right in front of you. Your airlines had them sent out overnight to me nearly three weeks ago. There must be some mistake."

"I'll check again."

"I don't understand this, Derek, I have been booking flights for years. This has never happened before."

"Well, honey, there is always a first time for everything. I'm sure they'll locate the problem. Here she comes again."

"Mrs. Callahan, I went back into my manager's office, and he also ran the information. Your reservation was canceled out of the system."

"Then un-cancel it. I have plans to be at home for Christmas."

"I am sorry, but we also checked availability, and the flight is booked, and so far, we already have ten standbys waiting. You can join the waiting list, and we might be able to get you on a flight by tomorrow night or the next day."

Tomorrow was Christmas Eve.

"But the chances are not very good for even that, and in your condition, sleeping in the airport might not be very healthy," the attendant went on to tell her.

"She's right, honey. You can always go home next year," Derek told her helpfully. "Why don't we go home and call your father so he won't be waiting around the airport unnecessarily." Derek took her arm to guide her back out of the airport.

Suspicion finally started sinking in, and Tracey pulled her arm away from Derek. Turning back to the desk, she asked, "Can your computer tell me just who or what canceled my reservation?"

The girl typed quickly into the computer and came back to Tracey, who already knew the answer just by looking up at Derek's pale features.

"Well, Mrs. Callahan, it appears Mr. Callahan canceled the flight and paid the cancellation fees."

"Thank you," Tracey bit out the words as she moved away from the desk angrily.

"Yes, thank you. Did you have to be quite so efficient?" Derek told the girl and, after grabbing Tracey's luggage, hurried after his fast-departing wife.

"Tracey!" he called after, her but she refused to turn, refused to acknowledge him.

"You know I only did it for the good of our marriage."

Response, raised eyebrows.

"Well, how are we supposed to give our marriage a chance if you pick the one most important family holiday to be apart?"

Response, a back turned on him.

"You know, you're going to have to talk to me someday."

Response, a shrugged shoulder.

"You know, Tracey, Christmas is a time of forgiveness."

Response, a finger in each ear to tune him out.

"Okay, Santa, I'm going to have to count on you," Derek spoke skyward as he finished the drive home in silence.

Tracey kept up the cold silent treatment for the balance of the day and through the night. The next day, while Derek left on some last-minute errands, Tracey helped Nellie prepare for the Christmas feast that was to be taken out to the ranch. She sat at the counter, putting decorations on the gingerbread men, and complained about Derek's high-handedness.

"I can't believe he went back on his word like that. He tells me I can go. Then he cancels my reservations."

"Well, he never actually agreed to your running away, did he?"

"I was not running away, I was—"

"You were trying to run away from making a Christmas memory."

"How did you know that?" Tracey asked this woman who had become so much like a mother to her.

"Because I've been watching you, and you allow yourself to bask in his attention and love, but when you think he's getting too close, you do something to pull away. Christmas, being the magical time that it is, tends to leave the most poignant memories, and that scares you because you do not want to have memories of one and not have more. But if you would just hold still long enough, you would know that's what he wants too."

"He wants the baby, so he feels he has to keep me. I don't want him like that. And besides that, I don't want him anyway. I mean who wants a man who would pull such a low blow?"

"Expression of love."

Just like that, her anger deflated. "Oh, Nellie, when they told me, I didn't know what to do—kiss him or kill him." Tracey laughed. "So I ignored him because that drives him crazy, almost as crazy as he makes me sometimes." Her eyes sparkled. "You should have heard him trying to get out of trouble."

"When are you planning on letting him off the hook?"

"I don't know. I am still mad at him, and it won't hurt him to suffer a little longer."

"It *is* Christmas, Tracey."

"I know, which is why I didn't kill him," Tracey told her as she finished the cookies and wandered into the living room to practice Christmas carols on the piano.

That was how Derek found her a short time later as he slid onto the bench beside her, wrapping his arms around her. "Miss me?"

She just looked from his arm to his face with a questioning glance and shrugged.

"Hey, be nice to me. I brought you an early Christmas present," he told her as he turned her around to see what was behind her.

"Merry Christmas, Tracey." Robert held out his arms, and Tracey jumped up from the piano bench and ran into those waiting arms.

"Oh, Daddy." Tracey had not seen her father since the wedding and hadn't realized how much she had missed him. As she snuggled into his warm embrace, she asked, "How did you get a last-minute flight? You didn't wait on stand by, did you? What are Ann and the kids going to do without you for Christmas?"

Robert ignored the first question and answered the second, "Ann, hubby, and children are all happily settling in at the Callahan ranch. I just wanted to come see you before going out there also."

"Ann, Ron, three children, and you? Six tickets at the last minute on Christmas eve?" Tracey pulled away and looked from one guilty man to the other. "You were in on this too? My own father? What is this? A conspiracy? Why are you always taking his side on these issues?"

"Now, Tracey."

"Oh no, that 'now, Tracey, be reasonable' speech is just not going to work. As far as I am concerned, you all can just go on out to the ranch and have a wonderful Christmas without me because I do not want to be around either one of you now. I bet this little game even includes all the Christmas presents that we mailed home will now somehow mysteriously appear at the ranch instead of your house." A quick glance at the men told her she was right. Now she was mad. She had been angry before but willing to forgive, but now, oh no.

Nellie chose that moment to come through the kitchen door. "Nellie, these two men are all yours. They will both be very happy to help you load the food into the car and escort you to the ranch. "And since I won't see you tomorrow, merry Christmas," she said as she gave the woman a warm hug.

"Aren't you coming too?"

"No, Nellie. I think I've had enough of the family for now. Besides, these two do better at talking to each other when I am not around." With that said, she left the room and ran up to her room. The slam of the door reverberated through the house.

"Well, isn't this going to be a fine Christmas. You two have anything more up your sleeves?"

"Nellie, I—"

Nellie just put her hands up to stop him. "You know, Derek, you may pay my salary, but I've been around you now over twenty years, and I can't rightly say I always understand what goes on in your head. I know that your heart is in the right place, but sometimes, I wish your heart would engage your head before you act. As for you, her father, she trusts you to be there for her. You might not have broken her trust, but you sure as heck bent it up a lot. Both of you have the next few hours to figure a way to get that unhappy young woman out to the ranch and back into the Christmas spirit." She shooed the men toward the kitchen, and when Derek would have detoured up the stairs, Nellie stopped him. "Leave her be. She was ready to forgive you once. She will again. But right now…" Nellie cringed as they heard more doors slamming. "Let her get most of it out of her system."

Derek swallowed hard. "Good idea," he said as he held the kitchen door open for Nellie to pass through. "Your daughter sure has one hot temper," he said to Robert as another crash was heard overhead.

"Got it from her mother."

"And you lived to tell about it?"

"Barely." Robert patted Derek on the back as he handed him one of Nellie's covered dishes. "Just barely."

An hour later, the house was quiet, and Tracey had vented all she could. She even came back to the reality that what they had done, they had actually done for her, but she was so tired of being manipulated.

Later, as Tracey wandered downstairs, the house was so quiet she realized that they must have even taken the dog, because at this time of night, Barney was usually found sleeping under the Christmas tree. With a sigh, she turned on the Christmas tree lights but left the rest of the house in darkness. Then she turned on the stereo and tuned it into her favorite radio station, which was playing nonstop Christmas carols.

The lights behind her reflected on the window as she stood there looking out at the moonlit waves crashing in fluorescent white to the sand. Slowly, she lowered herself to the floor, and as she sat there in front of the evidence of God's work listening to songs about his son's birth, she prayed.

"Dear heavenly Father, I ask you on this most holy of nights to forgive me for my show of temper and selfishness. I have always looked on Christmas as Jesus's birthday party, and my show of temper will spoil the party for my family who came down here to be with me. I will call them tomorrow and ask their forgiveness. Tonight, I will ask for yours. I ask this in Jesus's name. Amen."

She had no idea how long she sat there, but eventually, she noticed Derek's reflection had joined hers in the window. She should have been startled, but she wasn't. Somewhere deep inside, she knew he would be back.

Once he realized she had noticed him, he stepped forward and sat behind her, resting his head on hers, his hands on her shoulders. For a few minutes, he just sat there, inhaling her musky scent and savoring the feel of her.

"I am not sorry, you know."

"I know."

"I just wanted spend Christmas with you. Still mad?"

"You would deserve it, you know."

"Probably. But my intentions were good."

"You wanted everything your way."

"True, but you did bet me."

"What?"

"I had told you that the issue wasn't over yet, and you said, 'Want to bet?' And I told you yes. I was just dealt a better hand."

"You cheated."

"True, I hate to lose."

"So do I."

"See? We are the perfect couple."

"No, I see an incorrigible man."

"Who wanted to spend the holidays with his incorrigible woman."

There was no winning with this man, especially when her heart was telling her she was just where she really wanted to be. So with a sigh, she turned to face him and wrapped her arms around his neck. "Thank you for coming back, but do we have to drive out to the ranch tonight?"

Derek nuzzled the exposed neck. "I told Adam we would drive out in the morning, about six—after Santa, but before the children can beat us to the tree."

"Speaking of Santa, you have been a very bad boy this year. You will only be getting sticks and coal."

"Oh no, he already left me my present." He kissed her gently.

"Oh really? And what may I ask is that?"

"I peeked. He sent me a sexy little redhead that makes my head spin."

"And what makes you think that's for you?"

"I found her all wrapped up and tagged." He lifted her hand up and kissed her wedding ring. "It's almost midnight. Do you think Santa will mind if I open my gift?" He placed his hand on the zipper of her dress.

Gently, he lowered her to the carpet next to the Christmas tree and gave her what she had been running from—the most beautiful, unforgettable Christmas memory.

Finally, it seemed that the Christmas season's theme of peace on earth had finally come home to the Callahan household.

$\sim$

"The Lord gave us his most beloved treasure on Christmas Day—his son."

"It is fitting then that these two gave each other their own most beloved treasure—forgiveness and love."

"If it could only be Christmas every day, then we would have no more problems with these two."

"If life was that perfect, we would be out of a job."

"I could use a vacation."

"I would like to retire, but I don't think that either option is in our near future. We still have six more months of work to do."

"I know, but for today, we can take the day to go and wish Jesus a happy birthday. I think they'll be okay for today."

And for today, they were. Tomorrow would be a different story.

10

The year closed, and a new year began, bringing with it new hopes and dreams. Both Derek and Tracey planned for the future, but neither one discussed those plans with one another. When they were together, they stayed in the moment, only looking as far into the future as to the birth of their child.

"No, Derek, you are not making the nursery into a mini–sports stadium. Although my daughter may like sports, she will not like living in a dugout."

"But my son will. And the frilly, sissy stuff is not going anywhere near my son."

"Teddy bears?"

"Horses?"

"Cats?"

"Dogs?"

"Winnie the Pooh?"

"Pirates?"

"Mickey Mouse?"

"Cowboys and Indians?"

"Barbie?"

"Pokémons?"

"Noah's ark?" Tracey was running out of ideas.

"Noah's ark?" Derek looked at Tracey with a grin. "My son and I could live with that."

"Good, your daughter likes the idea too." She laughed as the baby did somersaults in her tummy. Derek placed his hand on her stomach and grinned. "Yes, my son does."

"What makes you think it's a boy?"

"Because God wouldn't be so mean as to keep me completely outnumbered and make me have to live with three bad-tempered women."

"Bad-tempered huh?" She hit him with a couch pillow. "I'll show you bad-tempered." She went to hit him again, and he grabbed the pillow and held her down on the couch while he smothered her with kisses.

"Excuse me, you two," Adam interrupted them from the doorway. "But I thought Amanda and I were coming over here to help you decorate the nursery?"

Tracey struggled to sit up, and as she brushed the hair from her face, she blushed. "We were, uh, just deciding on the final theme of the room."

"Sure, that's what it looked like to me—a deep thoughtful discussion."

"That's it exactly, so if you and Amanda will go away, Tracey and I can finish our discussion." Derek waved his brother away.

"Oh no, it's that type of discussion that got you into needing a nursery in the first place." Adam placed his two-year-old on the floor and let her run over to her aunt and uncle.

Derek lifted Amanda up onto his lap and accepted her sloppy hug and kiss before holding her as she bent to give

Tracey the same treatment. Then the inquisitive little girl found the open book on nursery themes.

"Noah's boat," she told her audience. She clapped her hands.

"Well then, apparently, we made a good choice if we have Amanda's seal of approval."

"That's my daughter, the final approver and the supervisor."

"Well, Amanda, why don't you take Aunt Tracey out to the kitchen and supervise the baking of some chocolate chip cookies while your daddy and I get down to some serious designing?"

"Okay."

"But, Derek." Tracey wanted to be part of it all.

"You'll get the final say-so in everything, okay? It's just that I get a craving for hot chocolate chip cookies when it rains."

"You get a craving for anything made with sugar, for any reason. You, husband of mine, have a terrible sweet tooth. Come on, Amanda, let's let the boys play." She held out a hand to Amanda, who eagerly jumped off Derek's lap to take it.

Adam waited until the kitchen door closed before looking at his brother with an eyebrow raised in question. "Well, how long as that been going on?"

"What? Kissing my wife? Adam, if you are questioning that, then it has been way too long between dates for you."

"Shut up, that's another subject entirely. No, I meant Tracey actually claiming you as her husband?"

At first, Derek was confused. Then he realized what Adam was referring to and smiled. "Well, other than formal introductions and the doctor's office, that was a first."

"I'd say you were making progress."

"I'd say that if we don't get started, then Tracey will have both our heads. Where's Jon?"

"I still say it's progress. He'll be here soon. Now what did you have in mind for the munchkin's room?"

Wanting something unique, the men began to plot, plan, and create. When the design met with Tracey and Amanda's approval, the three Callahan brothers began to transform the spare bedroom upstairs into a dream nursery.

One evening, a few weeks later, when Derek was working at the office on a special contract, Tracey walked around the now-complete nursery. She loved the room and the feeling of love that had been put into it. She picked up the teddy bear that had made a home in the light-walnut rocking chair, which had been placed by the light-walnut Jenny Lind crib. Sitting down, she slowly rocked as she described the room to her unborn child.

"Your daddy went all-out for you. You have every animal known to man walking in twos across the border that runs all the way around the room, just at the perfect level for you to see from your crib. Below the border, the wall has been painted in a cream color, and above the border is a beautiful soft sky-blue. I had a hard time with that at first, because I thought he wanted blue because he thinks you are a boy. He really just wanted a sky for you to look at. He even created puffy little clouds using cotton batting to complete the look. Now you may think your father is a little nuts—he is, of course—but this time, his heart was in the right place. Up in that little cloud over your crib is a shelf, and on the shelf are two angels. Your father said they are guardian angels. He even named them for you. One is Sid, and the other is Charlie."

Tracey looked up at the little angels and had to look again. It must have been her imagination, she thought, but she could have sworn the statues had been grinning at her.

"Anyway, my little girl, just wait until you see your toy box. Most kids have a few shelves or an actual box, but you have a minireplica of the ark. It runs the whole length of one wall and is about two feet tall. It comes out from the wall about a foot. This gives a wonderful 3-D affect to the painted portions your dad painted more than halfway up the wall. Now I wouldn't want you to think you are spoiled or anything, but the ark is already filled with stuffed animals.

It's a beautiful room, my little one, from the nice deep carpet for you to crawl around on to the stars that sparkle on the ceiling for you to look at when it's dark. You are one lucky little baby."

She continued to rock and gently massage her tummy until the baby fell quiet, and soon after, she fell asleep herself.

This is where Derek found her an hour later. With an indulgent smile, he bent and lifted her into his arms. As he turned to carry her out of the room, he stopped by the two angels. "Thanks for keeping an eye on my wife and our baby. They need you, you know." With a final nod at the statuary, he left the room and carried his wife to bed.

For the next two weeks, Derek had to work late on a new contract, and Tracey decided it was a good time to visit to her apartment to see what she might need because less than four months from now, she and the baby would be living there. The apartment, of course, was clean and aired out because Derek had a cleaning crew go in every other week, but she noted that it definitely no longer felt like home.

"I just need to be here a little more often," She told herself as she wandered around. She sat down on her bed and touched the fluffy quilt and hugged a pillow to her. The frilly room used to give such comfort. Now she felt as if she was in a stranger's home. She opened the door to the spare bedroom, the room that would be her baby's home away from home.

"I had not even thought about the fact that I would need a nursery here too. It's not as if we can move the furniture back and forth." She looked around at the familiar but unfamiliar room around her. Was that how the baby would feel being in her special room at her father's and then being here? "No matter how pretty I make your room, it is going to feel strange to you, isn't it, sweetie?" She rubbed her very round stomach. "How can I make this easier for you?"

Stay with her father, was Sid's simple answer.

Not an option.

Why?

Because if she grows up with us already in separate homes, she won't know anything different, and she'll be okay with it. However, if I stay, eventually, he will grow to resent me for tying him down. And if we divorce then, she'll not only be in the same boat she is now, she will also know what it was like to have two parents all the time and then will have to learn to do with one at a time.

The Lord would prefer a child to be raised by both a mother and a father.

She will be, just in different homes. So do you have any other bright ideas?

Not if you are not going to listen to reason.

Fine then, go away. I have some real thinking to do.

Stubborn.

I think I've heard that word used a time or two. At that point, Tracey ignored the little voice in her head and began to formulate an idea.

Every day after Derek left for work, Tracey left for the apartment. She was working hard. She wanted to surprise Derek. She was anxious to finish so she could show him.

However, she would get her chance sooner than she expected.

After two weeks of late-night bartering, the deal was finally closed, and Derek left the office in the middle of the day, impatient to get home to his wife. He missed their evening walks and talks because for weeks now, he had been so late that she would already be sleeping when he got home.

Nellie jumped when Derek reached around her to snatch a cookie off the counter, and he kissed her cheek, apologizing for scaring her.

"Is my wife upstairs taking a nap? Or playing in the baby's room again?" He headed for the kitchen door, talking through Nellie's words. "If she doesn't stop folding and refolding all those clothes, she going to wear them out before the munchkin can wear them." He was already gone before Nellie could correct him.

Derek ran up the stairs and checked the nursery first, then their room. When he could not find Tracey, he went back downstairs. He checked the den and then returned to the kitchen.

"Hey, I thought Tracey was upstairs?"

"You weren't listening. I said she was out."

"Out where? Did she say when she would get back?"

"She usually returns about five or so."

"What do you mean, 'usually returns'?"

"She's working on a surprise for you. She has been for the last couple of weeks."

"What kind of surprise would keep her out until five every day?" Derek asked suspiciously.

"It's not my surprise to tell." Nellie turned away from his probing look.

"Nellie, I sense something in your voice. Is this the kind of surprise that I will be overjoyed about or one guaranteed to tick me off?"

"Derek, please do not put me in the middle."

"That means I am not going to be happy. Nellie, where is my wife?"

"She's putting together a nursery for the baby." She answered reluctantly.

"We have a nursery for the baby? What are you talking about?"

"You have a nursery here in this house, but she wanted to surprise you with a second one elsewhere."

"Elsewhere?" Derek was puzzled, but for only a moment. "Her apartment. The little witch is at her apartment." He pushed away from the counter in anger.

Nellie grabbed his arm. "She is not trying to upset you. She honestly thinks she is doing something good."

"Something good? Going behind my back to her old apartment and making plans for a life away from here? Not even taking into account she's eight months pregnant and should not be doing this kind of running around?" Derek ranted and then stormed out of the house.

In a wise move to protect Tracey from Derek's wrath, Nellie went to the phone and made a quick call to Jon, whose work was closer to Tracey's apartment than Adam, who was at the ranch.

A pounding on the door brought Tracey out of the nursery to answer the summons. She did not have to wonder long who was on the other side. She opened the door to one very angry husband.

"Is this what you call giving our marriage an honest try?"

"Derek, calm down. I don't understand why you are so upset."

"I thought we were supposed to be working on making this marriage work. I tell you I love you and want you with me forever, and you refuse to believe me, but I figured over time, you would listen to me. I had hoped that you would come to your senses. Now I think you have lost it all together. You have not only been lying to me about working things out, you go behind my back to spend time in your apartment."

Tears burned Tracey's eyes and spilled over. "I just wanted to get a nursery ready for here too."

"Why?"

"Because when our year is up, the baby will need a place here too. So I thought—"

"That's the problem! You aren't thinking. Preplanning to leave is giving a lie to your promise to try to make things work between us. Moreover, if you are doing this to make me mad, you succeeded, but not mad enough now or later to let you and my baby go. Am I making myself clear?"

"Clear enough to every neighbor in a four-block radius, I would think," Jon said from the doorway.

"Get out, Jon. This is between my wife and me."

"Sorry, brother dear, I have orders from Nellie to protect Tracey from you, and I am more afraid of Nellie than I am of you." Jon closed the door and went over to Tracey, putting his arm around her shoulders. "You okay, princess?"

Tracey looked from one brother to another. She had hurt Derek again, but this time, she had actually been trying to do something special for him. "I am sorry. It wasn't my intention to make you mad. I was trying to create something special. But I guess I failed you again. No wonder you can't love me." With that, she ran from the room and locked herself in her old bedroom.

"Such finesse, big brother. Any stray dogs or cats you would like to kick?"

Derek ran a hand around the back of his neck. "Shut up, Jon. She says she's not here to make me mad but to give me something special. What would make her think that anything to do with ending our marriage, I would find even remotely pleasing?"

"Well, first off, if you didn't hear her, she does not believe that you love her, and I would think that she thinks that by getting ready to move out, you will feel less pressure and be happy to be done with this marriage."

"That is the last thing that will make me happy."

"Well, you don't have to convince me. You have to convince her." Jon nodded toward the hallway where Tracey had run.

"Maybe I should let her go. I have had eight months to get her to fall in love with me." He looked around the room. "And by her being here, I would say I have not exactly succeeded."

"So you're quitting? Willing to let the woman you love and your child walk away?"

"I am not quitting. I am just trying to be realistic."

"How did you become the owner of a multimillion-dollar company being so stupid?" Jon asked in disgust. "If you are not going after her, I will."

Jon moved down the hall, with Derek right on his heels, so close that when Jon came to an abrupt stop outside the nursery, Derek barreled into him.

"Wow," Jon said as he walked into the nursery and grinned back at his brother. "Sure, the woman has no love for you at all."

Derek followed Jon into the nursery, and it was almost like being home. Tracey had recreated his design for the nursery. "How in the world did she get that ark? It took three of us to put it together."

Jon had wondered the same thing and had been checking it out. "The sign on the back is from that custom wood furniture place downtown. She must have had it custom-made."

"I don't understand."

"She's trying to give your child continuity. Tracey is paying you a compliment on your design. She is trying to bring a little of your home into hers. She's trying to tell you, you thickheaded brother of mine, that what you want for your child is important to her."

"What about what I want with her?"

"If she did not care about you, why would she care about anything you want? You came here angry and refused to give her a chance to explain. This time, you owe her the apology."

Derek did not answer but went to the closed bedroom door and knocked softly. "Tracey, can I come in?" A soft cry answered him. "Please, Tracey, don't cry. I am sorry for yelling. Please open the door."

Turning around, he saw Jon sitting in the rocking chair, watching him with his arms folded. "Apparently, she's not talking to me."

"The least you deserve, big brother," Jon told him with a smug smile. Then he nodded toward the closed door. "You can either wait her out or pick the lock."

"You do have good ideas once in a while," Derek told Jon as he pulled out his pocketknife and went to work on the lock. It was only a few moments until he heard the lock click. Putting the knife away, he opened the door.

"Tracey, I'm sorry I yelled at you, but I am not happy about your being here working while being eight months pregnant. Besides the fact, I really don't like the idea that you are preplanning the end of our marriage. But I do appreciate the thought behind your efforts."

Deep breaths, as if trying to stop crying, was his only response.

"Come on, honey, give me a break here, would you?" Again, breathing was all he could hear. "Fine, I'll go out and sit in the living room until you get tired of being in here alone." Derek turned away but paused, waiting in hope.

"Derek," Tracey called out huskily from where she sat at the side of the bed.

"So you are speaking to me." He breathed a sigh of relief before answering, and he stepped back into the room.

"I guess I'll have to."

"Have to? I don't think I care for that wording, and I'll probably regret asking this, but why?"

"Because it usually helps for a woman in labor to talk to her coach and tell him exactly what she thinks of him for putting her in this much pain."

"What are you talking—" Derek began. Then her words hit him. "Labor? You're in labor?"

"That's what usually happens between broken water and birth," she informed him as she carefully got up from the bed. "I changed my clothes, but I don't think I'm up to driving myself to the hospital, so if you are done yelling at me, I will let you drive me. If you have more to yell at me about, I'll ask Jon. Because your daughter isn't messing around. These contractions started at about three minutes apart, so I don't have time to deal with you."

Derek ran over to her and scooped her up. "Are you okay?"

"Put me down. I am way too heavy for you to carry."

"You are still light as a feather. Besides, I like holding you in my arms." He grinned at her with a mock leer.

"Stop giving me a line, Casanova, and get me to the hospital," she told him as she felt another contraction begin. "Unless you guys want to have the baby here?" she added breathlessly to the two brothers.

"Oh no you don't. Get moving, Derek. I'll follow and call everyone on the way." Jon shooed them out of the door. He made sure that Derek had her in the car and had pulled away from the curb before he looked skyward in prayer. "Okay, God, here we go. Please keep Tracey and the baby safe."

"We have yet to fix these two, and here comes stubborn Callahan number 3."

"Hold on to your wings! Here we go."

11

Robert came down the hall, not quite at a run, until he reached the waiting room at the hospital. "Well?"

Adam and Jon looked up and shook their heads. "Apparently, this child of theirs is as stubborn and pig-headed as its parents."

"It's been fifteen hours. Everything is okay, isn't it?"

"Derek was out a few minutes ago and said everything was okay, just that the baby had started out fast and has slowed down."

"Is that normal? I can't remember it's been too long."

"It's not a bad thing, apparently, but it's not the normal thing, but then we're talking about Tracey and Derek's child."

The men shared a laugh, but as the next five hours passed, the men's sense of humor faded, and worry set in.

"Tracey, how are you doing honey?" Derek asked as he wiped her forehead with a cool cloth; the latest contraction had passed.

"Remember that truck that hit us eight months ago?"

"Yeah?"

"It came back for a second shot at me."

"Do you want me to get the doctor and have him order the epidural?"

"No drugs. I will not take any chances with our baby."

"They use epidurals all the time now. You heard the doctor. There are no side effects to the baby."

"No. I'll be fine, so stop arguing with me and put your coach hat on because you're on again."

Derek helped her through the next contraction and again soothed her afterward with a cool cloth. Now he understood why God chose women to procreate because it was killing him just to watch what she had to go through, and he wasn't even in any pain.

Another hour later, Derek made his way to the waiting room while the nurse was in with Tracey. All three men looked up as he entered. "Well?"

"Not yet. She's refusing the stupid epidural that would give her relief and rest. She's exhausted, and the baby's heartbeat is slower. The doctor wants to do a cesarean section, but she's holding out. The doctor said he would hold off only for one more hour—that is, *if* the baby's heartbeat does not fall any lower. They put Tracey on oxygen to help her and the baby." Derek looked at his father-in-law and his brothers. "I have never been so scared in my entire life."

Robert put his arm around Derek's shoulder as his brothers came around the other side of him. "She's going to be just fine, son. We must have faith in that." Robert swallowed his own fears to reassure Derek. Then all four men stood with their heads bowed and prayed together.

"Mr. Callahan, we need you right now," the nurse called from the doorway, and without a word, Derek turned and went back down the hall at a dead run.

"Is everything okay?" Robert asked the nurse, almost afraid to hear the response.

"Someone will be out to update you soon, I'm sure," the nurse stated as she left the area.

"Oh great, terrorize us, then leave us hanging. If this is not a test of our faith, nothing ever will be," Jon sputtered angrily and then the wait began again. It would be another half an hour before Derek would join them. Robert felt his heart stop beating when he looked up at the doorway to see his son-in-law standing there with tears in his eyes.

"Derek? Please…" Robert could not ask anything more, his fear choking the words in his throat.

Adam jumped to his feet, heading for his brother. "Tracey, is everything okay with Tracey?"

All three men held their breath as Derek wiped away the tears from his eyes and smiled. "Tracey is fine. She is waiting to show off our little surprise package. So come on, Grandpa, Uncle Adam, and Uncle Jon."

The three men were in such a rush to get down the hall that it wasn't until they walked into the room that they realized they forgot to ask if it was a boy or girl.

Robert was the first to get to his daughter. He hugged her to him tightly. "How are you? You look so tired, beautiful but tired."

"I'm fine, Daddy. But I sure understand now why they named that process labor." She laughed softly. "Don't you want to meet your grandson?" Tracey guided all three men's attention from her to the squirming bundle wrapped in a blue blanket, in a little crib with a warming light over him.

"So, Derek, you were right. It's a boy. Tracey's going to have a hard time living this one down." Adam grinned at his sister-in-law.

"Oh no she won't. My stubborn wife hates to lose, so she not only gave me my son, but if look to the other side, she also gave me a daughter." Derek stepped over to the matching crib on the other side of Tracey's hospital bed and lifted another little bundle, this one wrapped in pink.

"Twins?" Jon was the first to laugh. "You guys never mentioned twins!"

"We didn't know. Apparently, these two played a great game of hide-and-seek. Although it explains why the heartbeat would be so different from one visit to the next."

"Are they okay? They look so tiny."

"They are absolutely healthy, but little boy blue over there only weighs four and a half pounds, and the little princess here only weighs four pounds even. They are a month early, so the doctor feels they are actually a good weight. They are breathing without difficulty, but they will have a little problem with body temperature, so they will have to hang around the sunlamp for a while," he said as he kissed his daughter before placing her back under the warming light.

"Okay, all of you, you have had your visit. Now out. This little mama needs to get some rest," the nurse said as she entered the room.

"Hey, we just got in here," Jon objected, but he looked over at Tracey and knew the nurse was right. "Oh, okay, but beware, we'll be back." Jon gave his new nephew a kiss and then walked around the bed to his niece. He gave her soft little cheek a matching kiss before going to Tracey.

"They are beautiful. Good job, little sister." He gave her a quick hug and a kiss. Then the other men followed suit.

When Robert hugged his daughter, she grabbed his hand. "I wish Mom was here with us."

"She is, not like we would wish, but she is right here, loving you and proud of both you and her grandchildren. I love you, baby girl."

"Thank you, Daddy. I love you too. Dad, can you make sure Derek goes home? He's so tired, and the three of us are going to go to sleep now. Please pull rank and make him get some rest?"

"You know, I may be tired, but I am not deaf," Derek interrupted.

"Well, you need to go home and get some rest. For two weeks, you have come home late and gotten up early, and now today, please?"

"Now that everything is over, I'm fine. I'll watch over the babies while you sleep."

"Derek, you told me less than an hour ago that I could have anything I wanted. Did you mean it?"

"Well, of course, although I was under a little stress at the time."

"Well then, what I want more than anything else in the world is for you to go home and go to sleep and come back in the morning."

"But—"

"I promise you that we'll be still hanging around in the morning."

"But—"

Robert butted in with, "Derek, a promise is a promise. Are you going to tell me that you are going back on a promise to my daughter?"

"Oh, great, ganged up on again."

"It's okay, Mr. Callahan. I'll keep your little family safe until you return," the nurse assured him.

Derek sat down on Tracey's bed and pulled her up into his arms. "You call me if you need anything." He kissed her hard and deeply.

"Yes, sir."

"And whether or not you believe me, I do love you." He kissed her again. Then he kissed his children before leaving the room. He had to leave fast and not look back or he wouldn't be able to leave at all.

Robert kissed his daughter again and followed the three men out. Like Derek, it was either leave then or not at all, especially when he saw his daughter's eyes overflowing with tears.

The nurse bustled around, allowing Tracey the time to compose herself. "Sorry," Tracey offered an apology when the tears refused to stop.

"That's okay, honey, new moms do it all the time. Now these two little ones will be waking soon demanding food, so I would suggest you lie down and get some rest. Can I get you anything? You know the doctor left orders for pain medication if you should want it. "

"I wouldn't mind a little Tylenol, but I don't want anything stronger."

"Then Tylenol it is. I'll be right back."

After Tracey had taken the two tablets, she lay down, closing her eyes. First, she prayed and thanked the Lord for her two babies and asked him to watch over them closely. Then she prayed for Him to take care of her tired husband. "I love him, Lord. Please take care of him for me," she prayed.

At four o'clock in the morning, Derek thought he could sneak into Tracey's room and watch his new family sleep, but instead he found Tracey not only awake but nursing his son, his daughter sleeping by her side. The woman of his heart caring for the children of his dreams—what more could a man ask for? Nothing. "Thank you, Lord."

Tracey looked up at Derek as the door opened and smiled at him. "You are supposed to be sleeping."

"So are all of you. It seems that my daughter is the only one obedient out of the group."

"Don't bet on it. She was the first one awake, and she may be small, but she can be quite demanding." She glanced lovingly at her baby girl sleeping beside her then up to the child's father. "Just like her daddy."

Derek picked up his infant daughter and held her close to his chest. "And here I would have said that characteristic was more like her mommy." He lowered the baby back into her warming bed before sitting down on the bed beside Tracey. "So we'll have to debate that characteristic later, but I definitely know she gets her beauty from her mother," he told her as he bent to drop a kiss on her parted mouth before she could answer.

After thoroughly kissing his wife, he looked to his son and ran the back of his knuckle on the soft baby cheek. "You're a hungry little man, aren't you?"

"Yes, the nurse is pleased with both of them. I guess babies this small often have trouble nursing. Not these two, and she says if they keep this up, it won't be long before they're five pounds and able to go home," Tracey explained, with a tone that she hoped belied her underlying fear that something may go wrong.

"Tracey, don't lose your faith now. For some reason, we were chosen to bring these two beautiful babies into this world. The Lord worked awfully hard to make sure we had them. He is not going to let anything happen to them now. Have you been able to rest at all yet?"

"A little," she said, her eyes not meeting his.

Derek chuckled as he lifted his now-sleeping son and patted his back until he heard a tiny little burp. "Liar. I'll tell you what, little mom, I'll keep watch over these little bundles, and you get some sleep." Derek placed his son in his own little warming bed with a kiss and a cuddle before turning back to his wife.

"Deal?" He lowered the head of the bed a little and covered her up before he cupped her face in his hands. "Rest. You're going to need all the rest you can because if either one or both of these babies take after you or me, we are going to have our hands full." He kissed her then. As she would have spoken again, he put a finger on her lips. "Shh, sleep."

She was tired, so she gave in with a sigh and a kiss to his fingers before she let her tired eyes drift close. Derek quietly moved away to sit in the chair beside her. His eyes moved over his children, who were sleeping quietly; to his wife, who was now sleeping; then to his hand, where he could still feel the tingle of her soft butterfly kiss. His fingers curled into the palm of his hand, as if that would capture the feelings and the kiss for all eternity.

After two days, Tracey was released to a special mother's room, where she could stay with her children while they were waiting to get big and strong enough to go home with her. That would happen only five days later.

So exactly one week after coming into the hospital as a couple, Derek and Tracey left the hospital as a family.

Nellie had been to the hospital to see the two new Callahans, but she had been just waiting for them to come home, where she could be a part of their little lives.

"Derek, have you given Nellie the gift the twins decided she needed?"

"No, I was waiting for them to be home to give it to her." Derek grinned at Nellie's confused look. "Okay, close your eyes and no peeking. I know how nosy you can be."

"I'd take offense at that," the older woman began with a stern voice that turned to a soft laugh, "if it wasn't so true."

"So close your eyes," Derek prompted, and when Nellie complied, he went into the den and carried out a beautiful hand-carved rocking chair. He set it down in front of her and stepped back to stand by Tracey, lifting his daughter from her arms.

"Okay, you can open them now."

"Oh my," Nellie said as she reached out a hand and touched the chair, "it's absolutely beautiful." A word had been carved into the headpiece on the chair. She traced it with her finger. "Nana?" she asked, clearly puzzled.

"Well, sit down and try it out." Nellie sat, and Derek lowered his daughter into the older woman's arms, then knelt down beside the two of them.

"Nellie, you have been a part of my life almost since I can remember, and since my children are lacking an on-site grandmother on both sides, Tracey and I would feel honored if you would accept the position of honorary grandmother and let our children call you nana."

"Oh my," Nellie began as tears filled her eyes, blurring her view of the tiny, little bundle in her arms, "I never expected...why me?"

Tracey stepped forward and placed her son in Nellie's other arm as she too knelt down beside her. "I can't think of anyone more suited to the position."

"I can't think of a better position to be in." Nellie hugged the two infants to her. Simultaneously, Derek and Tracey got up in order to kiss Nellie's cheek.

So Kevin, named after Derek's father, and Julie, named after Tracey's mother, had come home.

It wasn't until later that evening when Tracey followed Derek upstairs that Tracey remembered that they had only been planning for one.

"Derek, we're going to have to—" She broke off as she arrived at the nursery. "You think of everything." The nursery now had two of everything.

Derek slipped his arm around her waist. "Not always, I should have asked you if I should have made the other room into a nursery so they could each have their own room. Also, I took the furniture from the apartment. I'll replace it later if the need arises. Okay?"

"That's okay. And about the second room, no, they need to be together, at least until their old enough to get on each other's nerves."

"That will never happen." He grinned as he guided her into their room, where two cradles were waiting for their new occupants.

Tracey lowered Kevin into his new bed with a last cuddle and kiss. "Bet me."

Derek did the same with Julie and then switched places with Tracey. "What makes you say that?" A kiss for his son was next.

Tracey ran her hand lovingly over her daughter's head and kissed the soft cheek before answering, "They are our children, aren't they?"

Derek pulled her into his arms with a laugh. "That they definitely are."

"Then they will fight." She put her arms around his neck.

"Yes, they will," he agreed, and as he nuzzled her neck, he added, "but then they will forgive and forget and become friends again."

"So that's the way it works?"

"Yep. Like her mother, Julie will make Kevin mad, and he will get angry and then he will forgive her and then forget it altogether, and they will play nice once again."

"Hey, that works both ways, you know."

"I have no idea what you're saying. I am sure my son will be just like his father and be the most easygoing and understanding of men because I would never set out to deliberately upset the women in my life."

"If that is true, then I brought the wrong man home with me, and you better leave before my husband gets home because he has a very nasty temper, a short fuse, and a very domineering personality."

"See? Like I said, perfect."

Tracey laughed. "I can't win with you."

"Oh, thank you, Lord. She finally sees the light."

"You're impossible." She pushed away from him with a laugh.

"Ahh, yes, but you love me anyway."

Tracey opened up her mouth to agree. "Y—" Then she realized what he said. "Y-your turn to watch the babies while I get a shower."

Derek looked at his children as the bathroom door closed. "I almost had her there for a minute. I'm going to need your help, you two, I'm running out of time, so rest up. We three are now on a mission, a mission to make your mommy fall in irrevocably in love with your daddy."

A few hours later, Derek rolled over in bed and pulled Tracey into his arms. Both babies had nursed and had gone back to sleep. Therefore, he had a few hours to have her to himself before it would be time to share her again. He kissed the top of her head. "I have missed holding you like this."

He felt a soft sigh against his chest before she answered, "Me too."

"Then will you make me a promise?"

"If I can."

"Please don't go back to that apartment. Please don't count the days to the end of our marriage. Don't preanticipate anything. Just let us be a family." He stroked her hair gently, letting the tresses fall through his fingers.

"We are a family, whether we are together or not."

"Tracey, please don't. I'm not going to blackmail you or bully you. I am just going to ask you for your promise given of your own free will."

Time seemed to stand still as he waited for her answer; he could feel her inner struggle. "I can try," came the quiet reply, and Derek closed his eyes, praying for guidance.

"No, Tracey, that won't work. Either yes or no."

Tracey looked over Derek's chest to where her children slept. He didn't want to let go of his children, and she didn't want to let go of him or them. Maybe she could just ignore their deadline for a little while, and maybe over time, he would want her for her and not because she was the mother of his children.

"All right, Derek, I promise."

Derek tipped her chin up. "Thank you." He covered her mouth with his with a kiss as if to seal the deal. "You won't regret it. That's my promise to you."

"No, Derek, you have never made me a promise that you haven't kept. Please don't start now."

He would have argued with her, but he knew for now that actions would have to speak louder than words, so he kissed her once more and settled her securely in his arms.

Silently, they both offered the same prayer, *Please, Lord, help us find a way to keep our family together.*

"Hey, how come we weren't privy to that little extra bundle of joy?"

"Remember, we are on a need-to-know basis. But I think the boss had the right idea."

"Other than that all his ideas are right, what's so extraright about this one?"

"With two babies to take care of, time will fly without a whole lot of time for trying to find loopholes or time to run away but with a whole lot of time for being a family."

"Ahh, yes. Now I get it. I guess that's why He's the boss."

"I wouldn't want it any other way."

"Me neither, me neither."

12

A promise was a promise on both sides, and for the next four months, their little family bonded. Derek was the perfect father. He helped with their baths and diaper changes. He got up during the night with them and walked the floor with one twin while she nursed the other and then vice versa.

When all the chores were done and playtime was over, the twins went happily to bed and left their parents alone, after six weeks, only bothering them once a night for a snack and a cuddle.

Derek and Tracey spent their alone time, talking about everything from what they could remember about their childhood, to what was happening at the office. They played the piano or just listened to music. They walked the dog along the beach or sat on the patio and watched the moon rise over the ocean.

When the doctor released Tracey back to a full life, they discovered a completely new appreciation of one another, a renewed way of expressing their love without having to express it aloud and face possible rejection.

Although the horizon had clouds on it, neither one of them looked to the horizon, so all was well, or it was until the view of the horizon was brought to them.

Tracey was just getting the babies up from their afternoon nap when her father walked through the door. "Dad! What brings you here?" She hurried over and gave him a one-armed hug and a kiss.

"I just thought I would surprise my baby and my grandbabies."

"It's a wonderful surprise. I'll tell you what, you take Kevin downstairs to play—he's been fed and changed—and I'll finish feeding and changing Julie. Then I'll bring her for you to play with too, deal?"

That was how they spent their afternoon. The babies, now almost four months old, showed off their skills with their baby gyms and used their gummy grins and baby giggles to keep the adults laughing. This went on until Derek came home from work; then he too joined the group until dinner.

After dinner, it was a family affair as father and grandfather took pleasure in working together in bathing the twins. Once Julie was bathed and dressed in a warm sleeper, she was handed over to her mother for her last feeding of the evening. Then the men went to work on Kevin, who, when ready, was in turn handed over to his mother.

When the babies finally settled down for the night, Tracey joined the men, who were sitting in the living room, both munching on some of Nellie's homemade cookies.

"I don't know why God gave men such good metabolisms and women such rotten ones. If I ate even a fourth of the amount of sweets either one of you did, you'd have to roll me around this house."

"You're just jealous because Nellie made my favorites and not yours," Derek teased.

"Of course I am, but at least I have a favorite. You like anything made with sugar."

"Well, actually, I do have a favorite, and it is sweet but has a lot of spice too, you know."

"Oh, and that would be?" she answered as she reached for a cookie despite her previous statement.

"You." He grabbed her and pulled her on to his lap, ignoring her squeal.

Robert picked up his glass of lemonade and sat back, wondering for just a moment if what he was about to do to this young couple was the right thing. His daughter was smiling and laughing as she played. Derek was grabbing her hand and stealing bites of her cookie to "protect" her from those unwanted calories. They were playing. They were a family, and what he was about to do could either solidify that or crush it.

But they are both going through life with the subconscious fear of not if but when the ax was going to fall. The Lord has given them all the guidance he can, but they have a right to their free will. The final choice must be theirs, and eventually, they have to face that. However, done the proper way, they are less likely to go in the wrong direction simply out of a sense of misguided hurt. You are going to do this out of love for them both. Stay firm. He never said loving and doing the right things would be easy. He just said it would be worth it. Sid and Charlie both could only help Robert find the strength to help this young couple because he too had his own will.

Robert opened his eyes to find both Tracey and Derek watching him. Tracey smiled at him. "Daddy, I think those two little monkeys tired you out. It's okay if you want to go upstairs and hit the sack."

"I wasn't sleeping, honey. I was asking for strength to actually get down to my real reason for visiting."

Tracey glanced worriedly at Derek before sliding off his lap and onto the couch by her father. "Is something wrong with you or Ann and the kids?"

"No, honey. I'm fine, and so is Ann and her crowd. I came here to talk to you and Derek." He reached beside the couch where he had placed his briefcase. Snapping it open, he pulled out a sheaf of legal-looking papers.

"As of Sunday, it will be a year from the date of your marriage. We made an agreement a year ago, and I am here to see that we follow through."

Derek and Tracey both spoke at once.

"Daddy!"

"Robert, please."

Robert raised his hand to stop them.

"The bottom line was that you two were going to give marriage a try, and if it didn't work out, then we would file the divorce papers. Almost four months ago, things were not yet working out. If they were, Tracey, you would not have been at your old apartment when you went into labor. And, Derek, you would have not been so crazy over it if you had been secure in Tracey's affections.

"So now it's time for truth and honesty. Either this marriage is real, and you want to go through eternity together, or it's time to part ways and go now while you are still friends and are able to give my grandchildren the best life possible with divorced parents."

Tracey was frantic. She had made the promise to Derek the night she came home with the twins, and she had kept it. She had actually come to believe that she stood a chance at someday having her husband want her for her.

Derek was just as frantic because this time, if Tracey ran away, he had no choice but to let her go.

"So I guess this all comes down to whether or not you two want to stay married to one another. Derek, do you want to stay married for now and eternity to my daughter?"

Derek looked at Tracey, whose head was bent and whose hands were clenched in her lap. She appeared to be holding her breath. "Yes, sir, I do." He saw her relax up until Robert asked the next question. "Why?"

"Why?"

"Yes, why? Why do you want my daughter as your wife?"

"Well, once you get past her stubborn temper," he began, hoping to make Tracey smile, but apparently, she was beyond that at the moment, so he continued, "she is warm and loving and caring. She is the mother of my children. We are a family."

Tears fell from Tracey's eyes. His answer had been honest, and she loved him even more for it, but it was not enough. She looked up at her father to tell him to file when she realized he was going to speak and ask Derek another question. "No, Daddy, please don't. That's not fair." She knew what he was going to ask, and despite her request, he asked anyway.

"But do you love her."

"Of course I love her. I have told her that, but she does not believe me, so I stopped telling her."

"Tracey, he says he loves you. Why do you not believe him?"

Tracey heart was breaking. She could not even look at Derek as she answered, "I believe he cares. I believe he loves our children. I believe he believes in his vows and the wishes of our Lord. He believes in family."

"But do you believe he loves you?"

"I believe he thinks he does, that he should because it is the right thing to do." She flinched as she heard Derek's fist hit the arm of the chair before he leaped to his feet. "What does it take to get it through your daughter's thick skull that I love her? I've told her, and I've shown her. What's left?" he ranted as he walked over the plateglass window and looked out over the waves crashing to the shore, crashing before his very eyes, like his marriage seemed to be.

"Calm down, Derek. Tracey, do you want to stay married?" Tracey was frantic; she couldn't lie, but she couldn't tell the truth and end up trapping Derek into a marriage he may regret later.

"Can you rephrase that question?" she asked quietly.

"No. Answer the question, Tracey. You have had a year to decide. Last year, you were adamant about getting a divorce. Do you still want the divorce, or do you want to stay married to Derek?"

"I'm sure that Derek would prefer—"

"No, Tracey, do not tell me what you think Derek wants. Tell me what you in all honesty want."

Tracey got up from the couch and would have gone to Derek, but he had turned from the window and was looking directly at her. "Yes, Tracey, I guess the truth is finally at hand. Do you want to stay married to me of your own feel will?"

Torn between telling the truth and doing what she felt was right, because either answer was bound to hurt.

Slowly, she walked to the door of the room, where, with her back to the men, she answered the only way she knew how, "Yes, Derek, with all my heart, I want to stay married to you, but I still want the divorce. File the papers, Father."

With that said, she ran out and up the stairs to close herself in her room. Once there, she fell to her knees by the bed and prayed as she cried as if her heart was being pulled apart.

Downstairs, Derek listened to her cry and wanted to go to her, but he had nothing to say. She had said it all. He felt defeated and walked to the nearest chair and dropped into it.

"I failed, and the worst part is I don't even know why. What kind of answer is that? She wants to be married to me, but she wants a divorce?"

"You haven't failed at anything. Neither has Tracey."

"Divorce is failure, and divorcing the woman you love is doubly so. I failed to make her believe I loved her."

"She knows."

"Yeah, then she must not love me."

"She does."

Robert smiled at his son-in-law, who was beginning to look at him as if he was crazy.

"Robert, I don't understand what you are talking about."

"You have told my daughter and showed my daughter that you loved her in one way. Now it's time to give her your love, but let her discover it on her own."

"I don't understand."

"Do you think Tracey loves you?"

Derek let his mind wander back over the last year. "I think she does."

"Is my daughter *in* love with you?"

"I just answered that."

"No, you did not. You can love someone in many ways, but being in love is something deeper and more meaningful."

Derek let the words float around his head for a moment, and finally, they made sense, and he looked up at the older man and answered honestly, "I don't know."

"Are you *in* love with my daughter?"

"Very much so."

"Then you need to let her go."

Derek was stunned; he had always thought his father-in-law was on his side. "I can't. I can't let her go without one more try." He started to get up to go to his now-quiet wife.

"No, Derek. Leave her alone. This has been looming on the horizon for a long time. This time, you both have to make some decisions on your own."

"Robert, you're talking in riddles now. Am I stupid, or is this not making any sense? Because I sure don't understand."

"Derek, without mutual love and trust in a marriage, you have no marriage. She does not believe you love her, and you have no idea if she is in love with you. Without the strength that knowing your spouse loves you with all their heart, then as in all marriages, when problems come, you will not have the strength to fight the problems together. Then eventually, the doubts will destroy what you have worked so hard to build. So I am going to ask something of you right now that will take all your strength and all the love you profess to have for my daughter. Are you up to it? Because what I am going to ask you to do has a foundation in the old saying 'If you love something, set it free. If it comes back to you, it's yours. If it does not, it never was.' Are you willing to take the chance? Is your faith strong enough?"

Derek's heart was pounding, and his eyes burned with tears of hurt and fear. "With the Lord's help," he finally answered and then he let his father-in-law tell him what he needed him to do.

Two hours later, Tracey left the sanctity of her room and went across the hall to the nursery, seeking the peaceful serenity that the babies offered her. "Tracey, can we talk?"

Tracey turned to face her father, who had been sitting in the hallway, apparently watching for her. "I guess. Let me check on the babies first." She went into the nursery and stood by each of their cribs, where they slept so peacefully. They no longer woke during the night, but she or Derek always went in at least once during the night to check on them.

When she came out, her father was waiting. "Let's go downstairs so we won't disturb Kevin and Julie."

"Dad, I can't face Derek right now."

"You won't have to," Robert told her as he turned and started down the stairs. "He's not here. He left for the ranch about an hour ago."

Tracey hurried behind her father; Derek had never left during an argument, no matter how many times she provoked him. She asked, "Why? Is he okay?"

"Tracey, you just told the man you want a divorce. You just lost the right to ask those questions." Tough love,

Robert reminded himself as Tracey stopped walking and looked at him in shock.

"Daddy, that's not fair.'

"Let's go sit down, Tracey."

She did, right where she was on the stairs.

"Okay." Robert shrugged, turned, and propped a foot up on the stair in front of him.

"You made a decision earlier tonight. However, I am going to ask you to do something for me before I file the papers for you on Monday. It is going to be the hardest thing I have ever asked from you. And you are going to hurt like you have never hurt before."

"There's a high recommendation for answering in a positive manner," she answered sarcastically. "Dad, have you been taking lessons from the Marquis de Sade lately?"

"Tracey, have I ever asked anything from you that you could not handle?

"Yes."

"When?"

"You asked me to give this marriage a year."

"And you handled it."

"No, I did not. I made a mess of this from the beginning."

"Or so you think, but now I am going to ask you to finish it. Willing to work with me?"

"Oh sure, why not? What form of torture do you want me to endure now, Marquis?"

"I raised such a funny, funny girl," Robert replied, then returned to the subject at hand. "Tracey, I am serious about this. This is your last chance to be honest with yourself and make truthful decisions that will affect you, your husband, and your children for the rest of your life."

"I understand, Dad."

"I don't think you do right now, but you will."

Two hours later, she was standing in her old apartment alone, crying and confused. "Not without my babies, Dad," she had cried.

"Tracey, if you and Derek are divorced, you will be without them 50 percent of the time. You need to understand that he will get the children either six months at a time, with visits every other weekend or every other week on both sides—something of that type. You will need to get used to them being away from you."

"But I am breast-feeding them still."

"You're either going to have to get used to a breast pump or wean them. For this weekend, I rented you a breast pump. Nellie will come by and pick up the milk tomorrow. You can use the pump before I leave, and that way, we'll have it for the morning. Tracey, you need to see what your world will really be like on those days when you will be in this apartment without your husband and without your children. You will have to live with your memories as well as your decisions. If they are the right ones, you will be just fine. If not, you are going to find it very difficult. You need to be sure, very sure, of all decisions you make, and you need to be alone to make them— no distractions, no influences. Just you and the Lord and your free will to make your own choices. Choose your own path."

Therefore, she found herself alone and wandering around the apartment. She had cried until she thought she had no more tears. She had talked to God for so long she was hoarse and then she cried again.

She could not even make it through one night without missing Derek and her children so much that she thought she was not going to be able to catch her breath again.

Nellie came the next morning to pick up the milk, and Tracey pumped her for news. "How are my babies?"

"They are fine. They miss you already, but their grandpa is keeping them entertained."

"Oh, Nellie, I can't stand this. I need to hold them."

"Tracey, you know how much I have grown to love you, but your father is right. You will be apart from your children half the time. You might as well learn how to deal with it now. Anyway, you'll be with them tomorrow."

Tomorrow was when her father wanted her and Derek to meet back at the house and finalize the details of the divorce. "Have you heard from Derek?"

"I can't discuss that with you. Remember, you are supposed to be trying on divorce for size."

"Yeah, well, I am not exactly crazy about the fit."

Nellie just smiled and gave her a quick hug. "I'll be back later for more."

Then she was gone, and Tracey was alone again. For the next twenty-four hours, Tracey lived with a movie reel of memories dancing in her head. Some made her laugh, some made her mad, and some just made her cry. "Where is my guardian angel now? You are supposed to keep me on the right track, give me advice, steer me right. Now when I need you the most, you forsake me?" Tracey called out into the quiet.

Free will. This decision is one that you must make on your own.

"But I don't want to be on my own. I need someone to tell me which road to take."

Silence was all she heard; apparently, she was on her own.

Derek paced the halls at the ranch and rode horses until he was exhausted and still could not sleep. Robert had been right. He needed to know if Tracey loved him or not. If she did, why would she want a divorce? If she didn't, why hadn't she just refused to be married to him altogether? She had to have known his threats were just idle ones. Her father was too good of a lawyer not to have seen to that. He knew the key was love and trust in that love, but he just couldn't put his finger on the answer. He was sure the answer was there, but something was keeping it just out of his reach.

And where are you, my guide? You always talk to me during times such as these. You always help me find perspective. Why are you silent now? Now when I need you the most.

Free will. Now you must find your way on your own.

But I need help. I need to understand. I need to know which road to choose.

Silence was all he heard; apparently, he was on his own.

Sunday arrived bright and clear, but Tracey had not even noticed as she pulled up to the house. However, as anxious as she was to see her children, she was afraid to face what was waiting for her inside. She was just as confused now, more so than when she left Friday night. Today was her anniversary, and she was going to go into that house that had been her home for the last year and finalize her divorce to the man she loved. It was too much for her, so she made her way around the house and down to the beach below.

Robert turned away from the window, having watched his daughter climb on to her favorite rock outcropping on the beach. "Well, kids, here we go. If this didn't work, I'm sorry," he told his two grandchildren, who just cooed contentedly, as if they were confident of the outcome. He wished he were.

When he heard Derek's car, he offered up one last prayer for God to give the young couple the strength to be honest with one another, then held his breath, hoping the Derek too would not want to come in right away and would choose to take a walk first.

"Thank you," he spoke to God as he watched Derek round the side of the house to make his way down the steps to the beach below.

Tracey let the salt from the sea spray mix with the salt from her tears as they ran unchecked down her cheeks. She couldn't believe she had any tears left. "I could have single-handedly solved the water shortage," she berated herself, but the tears still came.

Derek spotted Tracey sitting on the rocks and went to turn away, but he felt himself drawn to her once more. He too had no more answers now than when he had left on Friday. When he was within a few feet of her, he called out her name, so softly he wondered if she had heard him.

Tracey had felt his presence long before she heard her name, spoken so softly that she could pretend she had not heard it. However, the time for pretending was over.

When she turned and saw the shadows of tiredness below his eyes and the pain in them, she suddenly knew the questions that she needed to ask in order to choose the right path.

Derek waited for what seemed like an eternity, but finally, she held out a hand, and without hesitation, he accepted the first move. He took her hand and pulled her to her feet just long enough to pull her down to sit on the sand with him. He sat looking out to sea as she settled in front of him. She held herself away from him at first, then sat back against him, neither of them speaking at first.

"Derek?"

"Tracey?"

They both spoke together, and Tracey turned in his arms and placed a finger on his lips. "Please, before I lose my courage, I need to ask you a question. And I need you to answer me honestly. Please don't tell me what you think I want to hear."

"Ask me anything."

"Do you love me?"

"Yes, I do. I've told you that before."

"Yes, you have, but do you love me? Just me. Me, even if I had not had your children?"

"Yes. I love you, with or without my children."

"Are you sure? Why do you love me? What do you love about me? When did you know you loved me?"

Derek finally understood why she had doubted him. He hugged her closer to him. "Yes, I am sure. Why do I love you? I honestly have no idea. I just know I do. I love your smile. I love the feel of your hair when I tangle my hands in it. I love seeing it lying across my chest or my pillows. I love your eyes when they sparkle with laughter or darken when I make love to you. I love to hear your laughter. I love it when you challenge me. I even love it when we argue because making up is so much fun. I love your touch. It melts my heart. For this past year, I have not been just having sex with my legal spouse, I have been making love to my wife, trying to show her with my touch what she wouldn't hear with her ears. When did I fall in love with you? I have no idea, but I realized I was in love with you when you ran away from the hotel room in Las Vegas. If I had not been in love with you, I would not force you to stay my wife. I would not have annulled the marriage because of the possibility of a baby, which by the way I was right about, but I would have given you the divorce you asked for and accepted my responsibilities where they lay. However, I think I have been in love with you for a long time because for years, no matter whom I went out with, I compared them to you, and when they couldn't compete, I broke it off with them. Does that answer your question?"

Tracey's mouth had been open in shock as she listened to him talk. Now her eyes began to sparkle, and a smile began to form. "So let me see if I have this straight," she began. She tapped her chin with a finger as if pondering a serious thought. "You love me?"

Derek growled and turned her more into his arms. "Yes, what more do I have to—"

"Kiss me," she interrupted as she wrapped her arms around his neck. She was shocked when he pulled her arms away but held on to them.

"Oh no you don't! No distractions. If I start kissing you now, I'll never get to ask my own questions."

"What do you want to know?" she asked nervously.

"Do you love me?"

"Of course I do."

"And she says it like I should know this," he remarked skyward.

"I've loved you for years. Being married to you and having your children has been a dream come true."

"You acted most of the time as if was a nightmare come to life."

"Well…" she began, deciding to tease him first, "you were such a bully." She pulled a hand free and placed it on his cheek, needing to touch him. "I didn't want to be an obligation, someone you stayed married to only out a sense of responsibility. And if I wasn't who you loved, I didn't want to stand in your way of finding true love. I loved you enough to let you go. I wanted you to be happy."

"You know, we have spent a lot of time talking this year, but we sure didn't communicate very well."

"No, we didn't."

"Well, we are not going to make that mistake again. So I am going to ask you to explain the answer you gave your father the other night. Yes, you want to stay married to me, but you want him to file for the divorce anyway?"

"I had to answer honestly. Yes, for myself personally, I wanted to stay married to you forever, but as I said before, I did not want to tie you to me when I felt you were only staying with me out of a sense of duty."

"If he was to ask you that same question now, how would you answer?"

"I'd say yes. I want to stay married."

Derek reached into his pocket and pulled out a jeweler's box. "I ordered this when we were in San Francisco, and many times over the last year, I have wanted to give it to you, but the time never seemed right. I didn't want to upset you as I had done the afternoon in San Francisco, when I suggested buying new rings."

Tracey looked at him in confusion. "I don't understand."

"After you ran away that day, I still felt the need to give you a real ring, something special, so in this box are rings. I had designed to tell you how I feel about you, about us. Something you did not want to discuss up to now." Derek opened the box to reveal three rings—one sapphire-and-diamond engagement ring and two wedding bands.

Tracey reached out to touch the sparkling blue sapphires and diamonds that had been deeply set all the way around in the wedding bands of platinum. "Eternity rings," she whispered, in awe of their beauty.

"Full circle. As precious as true love," he told her as he lifted the engagement ring and the smaller of the two bands from the box. With his free hand, he pulled her left hand into view and removed the gold band. A ring in each hand, he looked at her, holding the gold ring out to her first. "A temporary ring for a time-limited marriage or"—he held up the eternity band—"will you be my wife for an eternity?"

Tracey reached for the second ring in the box and pulled it free, studying it thoughtfully for a moment. Then she looked up with her own question, "On one condition."

"And that would be?"

"Will you be my husband for an eternity?" She pulled the gold band from his finger and waited breathlessly for his reply.

"For now and for all eternity," he told her, and she slipped the eternity ring on his hand.

"And you?" he asked.

"For now and for all eternity," she told him as he slipped the rings onto her finger, kissing her hand once they were in place

"I love you," she told him as she placed her hand on his cheek, needing to touch him as she spoke. "I can't believe I can say that now, openly and aloud. I don't think I'm going to be able to stop telling you that."

"Good, because it's going to take a lifetime plus to make up for all the times I've been waiting to hear it. And now, the love of my life, you can kiss me."

"I can kiss you? You are supposed to kiss me."

"How about a compromise?"

"A compromise?"

"Yes, let's meet in the middle."

They met in the middle, giving themselves freely to the other. Unaware that the forgotten gold bands lay intertwined on the sand next to them. Forgotten for now, but later, they would put them in a box and keep them as a memory of how far they had come down the right path, the path God had wanted them to be on, together.

Robert gave Nellie a joyous hug, and together, they offered up a prayer of thanks before leaving their observation point and the two young lovers on the beach.

"Your mom and dad will be with you shortly. They're having a grown-up moment," Robert told his two kicking and gurgling grandchildren. "Give them a few of those once in a while, along with your love and prayers, and everything will be okay from now on." He kissed each of them good-bye. His job was done, for now. "But call me if they get out of hand again."

Epilogue

The children had been played with, fed, loved, bathed, and put to bed, and now it was grown-up time. Tracey had showered and changed before stepping out onto the balcony to join her husband.

Derek felt her presence, and without turning, he unerringly put out his arm and slipped it around her waist, pulling her close to his side. Tracey willingly let herself be pulled into his embrace because this is where she felt the safest. This was home; this was love.

"It's nice to be back home," Derek spoke quietly as he tightened his hold on her.

"I agree," she said as she turned in his arms until she could put her arms around his neck.

Derek looked down at her. "Never again, Tracey, promise me. Never again."

Tracey could not even pretend that she didn't know what he was talking about, and she shook her head slightly. "Did I tell you I threw away my long-distance running shoes today?"

"No, but I am glad to hear it," he said, and as her words penetrated, he felt the need to clarify the issue. "Long distance?"

"Well, of course, I have no desire to leave you for any reason for any great length of time. However..." She shrugged.

"However...what?" he wanted to know.

"However, a girl has to keep at least one pair of shoes good for sprinting."

"Why?"

"For the times that I make you mad—and I am sure I will—I may need a quick getaway, a short run to a safe place until you calm down."

"Plan on using those shoes often, my love?"

"I never really plan on making you mad. It just happens."

"That horrible black dress just happened?" he questioned.

"Okay, sometimes, there is a plan, but only when you are being a bully."

"I am never a bully. You only seem to have that idea when you are in the mood to disobey a direct order, one usually issued in your best interest. What if I ask to hang up those short-distance running shoes?"

"I would have to say that although I would like to think I will never have a reason to run for cover, that would not be very honest, so I would have to say my answer would be, 'Not likely.'"

Derek placed his forehead against Tracey's. "You are going to be a handful over the next few years, aren't you?"

"You can probably bet on it all the way into eternity," she said. Then she added mischievously, "Would you really want it any other way?"

Derek sighed and then smiled. "Probably not, but remember, I will always catch you."

Tracey put her hands on his cheeks, bringing his face closer to hers as she said, "I am counting on it, because you have my heart."

"As you have mine," he told her. He closed the distance between them and kissed her as the soft early summer breeze curled around them like a blanket of love, God's love.

In unspoken agreement, they sank down on bended knee to thank their Heavenly Father for his patience and the guidance that had kept them on the right path, the path that had led them to a stronger faith and to one another.

Derek rose to his feet, pulling Tracey up with him. "I will never be able to thank God enough for bringing you into my life. I love you," he told her.

"I finally understand the real definition of *soul mate* because you are definitely the other half of my soul. I am only complete when you are with me. I love you."

"As you are to me," Derek replied, and then with another thank-you sent heavenward, Derek took his bride of exactly one year into their home to continue their journey toward their heavenly Father, secure in their faith and in their love.

"It was close there for a while."

"True, but did you ever doubt the Father's plan?"

"Questioned it once in a while, but doubted it? Never. You?"

"Never."

And the stars in the sky sparkled just a little bit brighter as they reflected the joyous celebration of love felt by two successful guardian angels—Joyous, at least until they received the summons to report to the Heavenly Father.